The Viscount and the Wallflower

CHRISTINA DIANE

The Viscount and the Wallflower

Unlikely Betrothal Series

Copyright 2025 by Christina Diane

Edited by Emily Lawrence at Lawrence Editing

Cover Design by Erin at EDH Professionals

Beta Read by Rachel Word

eBook ISBN: 978-1-964713-05-2

Paperback ISBN: 978-1-964713-12-0

Contents

Dedication

Dedicated to those who refuse to change themselves only
to meet the expectations of others.

Note to Readers

Thank you so much for picking up my book—I'm truly delighted (and doing an undignified happy dance) that you're here!

Before we step into the historical world of Christina Diane, I wanted to share a little something about what to expect. While my books are set in the Regency era, I write with the modern reader in mind. You can expect stories that are character-driven, fast-paced, and heavy on the spice, with lively dialogue and plenty of heart.

I do my best to capture the setting and language of the time through research, but strict historical accuracy isn't my primary goal. Sometimes my characters insist on doing and speaking things their own way—and I let them. So, if you're looking for meticulous period detail and perfect historical precision, this book may not be what you are looking for (and that's completely okay!).

But if you're here for passionate heroines, swoonworthy gentlemen, witty banter, high stakes, high heat, and happily ever afters, all wrapped in a Regency-inspired world that welcomes diverse, bold, and intriguing characters—you're in the right place.

I hope this story sweeps you off your feet and carries you into a world of romance, tension, and a touch of scandal.

Much love and swoon,

Content Warnings

This book doesn't dive deep into the dark stuff—but you might encounter boundary-challenged relatives, over-sharing friends, and a generous dash of spice. I aim to flag anything that might need a warning, but if I miss something, send me a message so I can update the list for future readers. To keep this message spoiler-free, you can check out identified content warnings here: https://christinadianebooks.com/content-warnings/

Chapter 1

LONDON, ENGLAND - SPRING 1813

Lady Lily Fairfax braced herself for her mother's discerning eye as she descended the stairs of her parents' opulent London townhouse to attend her first ball out in society. She had made her bow before the queen, marking her as an eligible debutante on the Marriage Mart. So Lily would do as she was expected and she would attend the season with the intention to make an advantageous match with a gentleman of the highest title. At least that was what her father expected of her. Her father was an earl and preferred his daughter to marry a man of the same station or higher, but at a minimum a titled gentleman was expected.

Lily was nothing but practical and she knew she wouldn't be the type of lady that the pompous men of the *ton* wanted for their wife. She much preferred time spent reading a book or play as opposed to household matters, and she didn't have even the slightest interest in the latest fashions. If that weren't enough, her unfashionable red hair and light smattering of freckles on her nose and cheeks weren't what was considered beautiful in the eyes of society. Then, when you added her gold-rimmed spectacles, which she needed if she were expected to see far away without everything turning fuzzy and blurry, she would be overlooked for one of the more fashionable beauties seeking a husband.

So, in her mind, it went without saying that she would not command the attention that a diamond of the first water would, or even as much as the debutantes a few rungs below that. Lily figured it was their loss as she quite liked the way she looked. When she looked in the mirror, she just saw herself, a lady who loved the written and spoken word, had a sharp wit, and understood the way of the world from watching it. She couldn't look like or be anyone but herself, even if that meant she would end up a spinster, to her father's disappointment.

If nothing else, she had her books and her plays. The thing she most looked forward to about being out in society was going to the theatre, so she might see some plays she had read so much about. She was enamored with the display of passion and emotion from the works that she had read, particularly from Shakespeare. Stormy Wells, a torrid playwright who had taken society by storm, was all abuzz in the news sheets. She hoped she would get to experience one, or all of them, for herself.

As Lily made her way down the last few steps to meet her parents, her confidence wavered. It was one thing to feel confident in one's own home, but was quite another to be out in society where everyone seemed to have opinions and rules for everything. It baffled her how their society lived by a system where women were property and pompous men continued to decide what was acceptable behavior for all. How convenient that it was acceptable for men to attend brothels and keep mistresses, but women must be pure and devoted to their husbands.

"Lily, really?" her mother called out. "Give me the spectacles."

"Mama, don't you wish me to be able to see the gentlemen?" Lily knew it was too much to hope that her mother might ignore them. She should have tucked them in her reticle and then put them on once they arrived.

"You will see well enough without them. And you can make use of your quizzing glass if the need presents itself."

Lily huffed and tucked her spectacles in her reticule, hoping that would appease her mother. Her parents meant well. They cared about her, she supposed, but they were products of their society. They cared most about titles and social standing. Lily's younger brother would be the next earl, and it was her responsibility to marry well to further the family's connections. Or some such shite that Mama had told her more times than she cared to count.

"There, much better," her mother said. "Perhaps we should have powdered your hair."

"We must leave if we don't wish to sit in the carriage for an hour from the traffic," her father said, tapping his foot as he checked his pocket watch. He wasn't the kind of man that one typically said "no" to. When he wanted something, he typically got it, either by intimidation or throwing money at them.

For once, her father's impatience would work in her favor. She would much rather cause a scene in their foyer than have her hair powdered. It wasn't like the gentleman who married her wouldn't find out she had vibrant red hair.

They departed and boarded their carriage with no further primping and assessing of Lily's assets. At least, that's what her parents believed were her assets. She would argue that her ability to read and comprehend any text with ease, memorize plays, and to speak multiple languages would be assets, but what did she know? Nothing, it would seem in the eyes of society, which was certainly more their problem than it was hers. Not that anyone cared she thought so, as she wasn't the one who made the rules.

Once they arrived at the Fletchers' ball, they greeted their hosts and then were announced into the ballroom. She collected a dance card, and then her mother helped to place it on her wrist. There were fans fluttering everywhere from the other young ladies on the Marriage Mart, excited for the first ball of the season. Lily fought not to laugh at the display and wondered how effective the fans were in catching a man's attention.

She followed her mother to where some of the other matrons had gathered. She had already met all of them when they visited during the calling hour, so she offered her best curtsy when they greeted her. They spoke of some of the beautiful debutantes and who they believed would make grand matches. It wasn't lost on her that none of them deigned to compliment her appearance. Not that she required their hollow words, but she would have thought social protocols might have warranted as much.

The entire evening passed by at a snail's pace. Not a soul asked her to dance, and she wondered if she had somehow disappeared from view for all the gentlemen since they didn't glance in her direction either. Although she supposed she didn't bother to acknowledge them either.

Her mother made a few introductions, but each gentleman had to speak to someone about a matter of import, or something of the like. They could at least get more creative with their excuses to escape her presence without asking for a dance. Mama simply reminded Lily that she needed to smile and appear approachable as if she were the one who did something wrong.

If she put all her self-worth on how popular she was within society, she would be at rock bottom by then, throwing herself onto the floor with no will to go on. But she was her own source of strength and contentment and used the time spent ensconced against the wall, pretending to watch the dancers while she did a few complex calculations in her head and recalled some of her favorite Italian poems from memory. When it was time for supper, she mentally acted out a few of her favorite scenes from *A Midsummer Night's Dream* in her head while she ate. She was reciting some of Puck's lines to herself when her mother informed her they were ready to depart.

They wouldn't stay for the rest of the ball. Thank God for small favors. She flashed a victorious grin at her mother and then followed her parents out to wait for their carriage. Once they had settled into their squabs, she knew it was only a matter of time before one of her parents commented on her lack of success, so she stared out the window and waited.

"Did you meet anyone of interest?" her father asked.

"She didn't dance a single time," her mother said, her tone one of annoyance and contempt. Again, making it appear as Lily's fault that a gentleman didn't ask her to dance.

"Not at all?"

She almost took it as a compliment that her father was surprised. Then she thought that she should contemplate what a sad state of affairs that was.

"If you don't catch a man's interest during the season, I will make an arrangement," Papa said, confirming that there was no compliment intended.

"I am sure I will meet someone at the next ball," Lily lied. She just didn't want her father to play matchmaker or her mother to get any ideas about powdering her hair again.

The next few balls were much the same. Lily dressed in the most fashionable dresses, according to her mother, and spent her evening as a wallflower. Worst of all, in her mind, was that she had made no friends. The other debutantes either didn't take notice or perhaps wished to avoid catching whatever misfortune they believed had landed her on the wall.

She fiddled with her spectacles as she watched the dancers at Lady Harrowby's ball and recalled lines from Hamlet that evening. She glanced down the hallway that was within her view from her place alone and saw a handsome gentleman appear from one of the rooms, adjusting his cravat as he returned to the ballroom. A couple of seconds later, a blond woman appeared from the same room and caught Lily's eye as soon as she emerged.

Lily's eyes widened, not sure how to react. The woman smirked at her and started straight for her. Lily swallowed hard, trying to decide what she would say. Did she pretend she didn't witness them leaving their tryst in the middle of a ball?

The woman came to stand by her side. "You can keep a secret, can't you?"

"What secret?" Lily asked, giving her a knowing look.

"Exactly," the woman said. "I don't believe we have met."

"Lady Lily, the Earl of Fairfax's daughter," Lily said, giving a small curtsy.

"Lady Preston," the woman returned. "But I shall call you Lily, and you shall call me Rosina. Friends can dispense with the formalities, can they not?"

Lily wasn't sure that witnessing the woman's dalliances made them friends, but she wasn't in the position to turn down even the hope of having someone interesting to talk to.

"Of course," Lily replied. "If I had the luxury of disappearing for a while, I might do so. These things are rather dull."

Rosina laughed, then snapped her hand over her mouth. "I thought I was the only one. Do you see the way these debutantes act like this is all they live for? It makes me quite glad that I married and didn't have a season."

Lily's eyes grew wide at the realization that Rosina had a husband.

Her new friend noticed Lily's reaction and spoke again quickly. "My dear husband passed away. I have decided that I am open to making new...acquaintances."

Lily noticed the pain in Rosina's eyes. "I am very sorry about your husband," she said, offering her a small smile. She thought a subject change might serve Rosina well. "Perhaps that is why I haven't danced a single time this season. Not enough fan fluttering, I imagine. Is the flutter supposed to wave the gentlemen to them?”

Rosina laughed again and gripped Lily’s arm to steady herself. “You are far too interesting for any of these idiots. Well, not all of them are so bad. I shall introduce you to the best people of the *ton* to befriend.”

Lily cringed as her mother approached.

“Lily, stand up straight,” her mother admonished, then positioned her shoulders where she wanted them. “And try to smile, dearest. You want to appear approachable.”

“Mama, have you met Lady Preston?” Lily said, hoping her mother would realize she was being quite rude not addressing her.

Her mother realized her error and Lily almost laughed at the light shade of pink that reached her mother’s cheeks. “My apologies. I’m not sure where my head is. It’s so taxing with a daughter on the Marriage Mart. It is good to see you out of mourning, my lady.”

“Thank you, my lady. Your daughter and I have become fast friends. She is one of the most lovely young ladies out this season.”

Lily fought not to laugh at her mother’s reaction, unsure what to say in response to such a compliment to Lily.

“Indeed. She is sure to find her match soon.”

Lily knew her mother didn't believe that in the slightest. To her good fortune, one of the matrons waved her mother over, and she excused herself.

"Your mother is quite overbearing," Rosina sympathized.

"You didn't have to compliment my appearance, Rosina. I am far from the beauty these titled gentlemen shall set their caps at."

Rosina pulled Lily's arm so that she faced her. "None of that talk. You are unique and quite beautiful. I imagine that red hair of yours is quite eye-catching in the sun. Don't let anyone compare you to the young misses who all look the same. When you meet the right gentleman, he shall take notice, and you shall be the only person he will ever have eyes for. Who cares if you dance with one or a hundred gentlemen? Only that one shall matter."

Lily decided not to point out that it was easy for Rosina to say such things when she had blond hair and perfect skin—and had already been married once before.

"I shall think about what you said."

"You just need to be around others that appreciate you. You appear more approachable when you are afforded the opportunity to be yourself. I am going to make sure you are invited to the Ockhams' house party at the end of the season," Rosina said, clasping her hands together in excitement. "I'll convince your mama to let me be your chaperone. We must get you out of these dreadful ballrooms."

Lily would enjoy the opportunity to be away from her parents and perhaps meet other interesting people. "I would appreciate that if it isn't too much trouble."

"Nothing is too much trouble for my friend. And now you will have me to spend time with at these events." She paused and glanced around them. "When I'm not otherwise engaged."

"Is it too forward for me to ask questions about your…engagements? Mama won't tell me anything about what to expect when…" Lily let her words trail off, assuming her friend would understand her meaning.

A playful smile appeared on Rosina's lips. "I shall answer any question you wish."

"I am going to hold you to that. Perhaps we shall take tea together soon."

"I'm going to attend the theatre tomorrow. Would you like to join me? Your mama might let you attend without her since I am eligible to be a chaperone. You could join me for dinner at my townhouse and then we could attend together. It would be so much fun."

Lily fought to keep from letting the depth of her excitement show. Going to the theatre with a friend would be an absolute triumph compared to the insincere pleasantries and forced enthusiasm of yet another tedious London ball.

"That would be wonderful. I believe *Duke About Town*, the newest play by Stormy Wells is playing, is it not?"

"You are correct. Do you follow the theatre?" Rosina asked.

"I do as much as I can, but I've never seen a performance before. It would be such a delight to see one of Stormy Wells' plays."

Rosina looped her arm in Lily's. "Then come with me to find your mama. I will arrange everything."

Lily might not have succeeded in landing a husband, but as far as she was concerned, the season was looking up.

Chapter 2

"You will leave the party betrothed to Lord Knox."

Her father's words had played in Lily's mind over and over since she arrived at the house party hosted by Viscount and Viscountess Ockham. Her father was quite clear in his intention to see her wed to the man, and he knew there was a slim chance that she could refuse. It wasn't a request or a suggestion. It was a command. Lord Knox apparently expressed interest in her after a conversation with her father, and if he wished to marry her, it appeared her father would have the contracts ready.

House parties were known for sparking proposals, but typically from passionate couples, taking advantage of the opportunity to give in to their desires while being in close proximity for a fortnight. Or more accurately, being caught in the attempt to do so.

Lord and Lady Ockham had invited around thirty guests to their party, so the house was sure to be lively. Lily wasn't certain if she would find herself announcing a betrothal, but given how her father already put it around town that she was being courted by the earl, it was another nail in her coffin, so to speak.

She wouldn't meet Lord Knox until she joined the other guests for dinner. She hadn't met him during the season because he rarely frequented *ton* events. Lily supposed that was a point in the man's favor.

When her father told her she must marry Lord Knox, she wondered what her father might have promised the man. She'd never even seen him, nor did she know anything about his character.

The man didn't even come to meet her when he discussed the matter with her father at his club. Would it have taken that much time to at least call on her and meet her in person? Her father said he was only in town for a couple of days, so the courtship would wait until the house party.

Lord Knox was an earl, which would at least equal her father's rank. She had heard neither concerning nor good about him as the man didn't spend much time out in society. Which was a point in his favor, but it meant she had nothing to go on. Rosina hadn't even met him to have a measure of what kind of man he was.

It wouldn't matter if she wished to marry the man or not. If he asked, her father would accept on her behalf. He already said as much. That was another point in the earl's favor, that he didn't just make the arrangement with her father and the matter of business settled without meeting her. Her father agreed to her request to attend the party with her maid and Rosina as chaperone, with the understanding that the man would court her while there.

Lily had agreed to what she must in order to attend, but she hadn't actually been certain whether she would entertain the notion of a courtship with the earl or not. Although there was still the chance that once he met her and realized she wasn't a darling of the *ton* that he would lose interest, and her problem would go away. Then she could go on about her business and enjoy the house party.

Although, what if he was a total beast? She wasn't shallow enough to expect him to make her heart stop when she met him, but she wondered what he might look like. What if he had a horrible personality or was the type of man who would be cruel to his wife? She wasn't certain any of those things would sway her father from the match, which was the sad state of things for women in society.

She sighed at the notion, hating to admit that she was more nervous than she expected to meet him. Glancing at the clock on the mantel, it was almost six, and her hostess wanted everyone downstairs at six sharp. She knew enough about the fierce Lady Ockham to know she didn't wish to be on the woman's bad side.

Lily departed her chamber and made her way downstairs and joined the guests who had already gathered. She found Rosina and joined her side.

"Have you figured out which one he is yet?" Lily asked.

"Not yet, but once our hosts greet us, we shall ask for an introduction."

A handsome man strode into the room, and Lily couldn't help but take notice. She hadn't looked twice at most of the gentlemen during the season because their pompous, arrogant attitudes made them wholly unattractive, whereas the other debutantes only waved their fans faster in their presence.

Although, a fan might have been helpful at present to cool flushed cheeks. Perhaps the fans made more sense after her reaction to whoever the gentleman was. He had dark, chestnut hair that was a bit longer than was acceptable for gentlemen. Almost rakish in his looks, but he didn't carry himself like a rake. She couldn't see his eyes, much to her disappointment, but she took notice of how finely his clothing was cut to fit his taut form. His shoulders were broad and, for the first time in her life, she noticed a man's thighs. How had she not looked there before? Because on that man, they were beyond enticing.

It wasn't just this man's looks, which were indeed quite attractive, but there was something else about him. She couldn't quite place her finger on it, but she found him intriguing. What if he could be Lord Knox? That would just be too perfect. A girl had seen a boy across the crowded room and the boy turned out to be the very one supposed to be courting her. Sounded just like something Stormy Wells would write, only he would add a bit more flair.

"Rosina, do you know who that is? Perhaps it's Lord Knox."

Rosina looked at the man and frowned. "Sorry, but I know that gentleman. That's Viscount Callan."

Lily should have known better to think things would work out in such a fantastical way. If a play were to be made about that encounter, it would be a tragedy. One where her character was the ironic, witty spinster, and the handsome gentleman married some other young lady who batted her lashes and drove him to distraction. The story wrote itself.

Besides, why would a handsome man like him need to arrange a courtship through her father instead of attending the season and selecting a bride for himself? A troubling thought crossed her mind.

"Has he been one of your…engagements?" Lily asked. It would be quite awkward if she had contemplated a man that her friend had bedded.

"No, he's not my type."

Lily laughed. "Handsome and titled isn't your type? I beg to differ."

Rosina nudged her friend. "My type is men who don't wish to marry. And I haven't heard him declare as much."

"So he is seeking a wife?" Lily wasn't certain why she was asking, but she couldn't stop herself.

"I suppose I don't know, actually." Rosina smirked at her. "Are you trying to suggest him for me?"

"No, not at all," Lily said, much faster and more intently than she should have.

Rosina arched her brows and patted Lily's arm. "I see. This might be an interesting party, indeed."

"It's not that. Oh, never mind." Lily huffed. Perhaps it was that. Not that it mattered. With the viscount's obviously handsome masculine features, he would be the type to chase after Rosina or one of the other ladies, but not her. The sooner she met Lord Knox, the better.

Lily noticed her friend was watching another gentleman she didn't know. He was also quite handsome. Was it a rule that only handsome men were invited to this party?

"And who are you staring at?" Lily asked.

"That is the Duke of St. Albans," Rosina replied, not taking her eyes off the man.

Rosina only had a couple of men with whom she had "engagements" as Lily always referred to them, but the *ton* found out when her last gentleman told others about their involvement. Rosina shattered his poor heart when she refused to marry him, and he set out to ruin her. Which only proved why Rosina was right to reject the man's proposal.

But since society was quick to believe a man's word, the gossip mongers made it out as if she took a different man to her bed every night. It wasn't as scandalous as all that, and Lily commended Rosina's resolve not to marry when she didn't wish to do so again. Rosina was three-and-twenty and a wealthy widow, so she had the freedom to do as she wished.

"You seem taken with him," Lily said, eyeing her friend.

Rosina waved her off. "This is his first event in society, other than casual appearances, where his attendance was required. He would make an intriguing friend."

"Intriguing, indeed."

Rosina glanced at her that time and opened her mouth to offer a retort but closed it again when their hostess approached them.

"Are you both having a pleasant time so far? Dinner should be announced soon," Lady Ockham said.

"We are, my lady," Rosina said. "We hoped you might introduce us to Lord Knox as we aren't certain who he is."

Their hostess nodded in understanding. "I believe I heard something about him courting Lady Lily," she said, giving Lily a kind smile.

"At least that is what my father's intentions are," Lily replied, fighting an eye roll.

"Well, come with me. I think I see him among some of the other guests. You probably couldn't see him from here."

The ladies followed behind Lady Ockham, moving through a group of guests until they reached a gentleman standing near the sideboard.

"Lord Knox," their hostess started, "please allow me to introduce Lady Lily and Lady Preston."

"My ladies," he said, bowing to them. "Pleased to meet you both."

His appearance surprised Lily as she found him quite handsome. Not so much as Viscount Callan, in her opinion, but that was of no matter. He had brown hair, but some strands almost appeared gold. A gentle kindness shone through his eyes, which were a deep blue. He had a perfect aristocratic nose and broad shoulders. She dared to glance at his thighs, and they didn't appeal to her the same way that Viscount Callan's had.

He took Lady Lily's hand in his. "I hope you might allow me to spend some time in your presence over the next fortnight."

"We shall let you two get acquainted," Lady Ockham said, looping her arm in Rosina's as they moved on to another group of guests.

"I should like that, my lord," Lily said, replying to his earlier request.

"Tell me some things you enjoy."

She grinned at him, pleased that he asked about her before telling her all about himself. "Well, I enjoy reading, maths, museums, art, and the theatre."

"The theatre?" he asked. "Have you been to see a play yet?"

"Oh, yes! Rosina, Lady Preston, she has a private box, and I have gone several times with her during the season. The first show we went to was *Duke About Town*. It was so witty, with such a romantic ending. There is nothing better than attending the theatre. Don't you agree, my lord?"

He appeared distracted, and she wasn't certain if he had heard her.

"Um…yes."

She almost questioned him about it, but Lady Ockham appeared again.

"My lord, my lady. Please allow me to make my friend, Lord Demming, known to you both. Marquess of Demming, this is Lord Knox and Lady Lily."

Another handsome man, Lily thought. Surely it had to be a requirement when Lady Ockham made the guest list. She might believe so if their hosts weren't famously a love match and prone to displaying their affection in front of their guests.

"It is a pleasure to meet you both," Lord Demming said, bowing over her hand and then nodding to Lord Knox.

"You as well, my lord," Lord Knox said.

"Hopefully," Demming started again, "I shall get to know both of you better during the house party as I am sure we will partake in many of our hostess' activities together."

Lord Demming seemed like a kind man, and Lily found she already liked him very much. He wasn't as stuffy as some of the other gentlemen she met during her season.

"I look forward to it, my lord," she replied.

Dinner was announced, and Lord Knox extended his arm to her. She accepted it and allowed him to lead her to the dining room. He seated her and then took his own seat at the other end of the table.

The meal was served, and dinner passed with casual conversation all around her. She mostly listened, and no one asked anything of her. She wished Rosina had been seated nearby so she would have had someone to speak with.

Once the meal ended, the ladies returned to the salon while the gentlemen enjoyed their port and she rejoined Rosina.

"What do you think of Lord Knox?" Rosina asked. "I've been dying to find out. He is very handsome."

"He is," Lily replied. "And he seems nice enough, but I know nothing about him yet."

"You shall have many days to learn about him. Just be yourself and remember what I said the night we met."

Lily had thought about her friend's words many times. She just wasn't convinced that it would happen for her.

"And what about you and Lord St. Albans? I saw you speak with him."

She thought she might have seen a bit of blush on her friend's cheeks. "There is perhaps a chance we might get to know each other better as well."

"Do I get to hear all about it?" Lily asked.

"But of course," Rosina replied, looping her arm in Lily's. "I can't believe your mama lets you be my friend with my scandalous influence."

Lily laughed. "You are well connected and are the Dowager Marchioness Preston. That is all my mother needed to know."

A couple of other ladies joined their group, and they spoke of many varied topics until the gentlemen joined them in the salon.

"Are you enjoying the company of the other ladies?" Lord Knox asked, catching her attention.

"I am, my lord," she replied. "It seems none of the gossips and more discerning members of the *ton* are in attendance."

He patted his chest with a dramatic flair made for the theatre. "Well, that is quite a relief."

She couldn't help but laugh. "You jest, but it is. I might even get to have an intellectual conversation without being called a bluestocking."

"What is it you are most interested in discussing?" he asked, seemingly interested in her response.

"I mentioned earlier how I love reading and the theatre. So I always enjoy the opportunity to discuss those things."

Rosina always tired quickly from her speaking at length about such things.

"And do you have a favorite play?" he asked.

"I can recite most of Shakespeare's plays by heart. I'm not certain I could select a favorite. I enjoy both tragedies and comedies, so that doesn't help me narrow down my choice. I also relish the plays by Stormy Wells. The way he evokes such emotion in the dialogue draws a person in."

"If you will excuse me," Lord Knox said suddenly. "I am going to take in a bit of the night air."

He had done the same thing again. The man asked her a question and it appeared that he wished to hear her response. Then it was as if he forgot he was engaged in a conversation.

"Did I hear that you enjoy the theatre?" a rich baritone asked, pulling her from her irritation at Lord Knox.

She turned to see who it was, and Viscount Callan stood beside her. Her breath caught for a moment, but she recovered and turned to face him. "Indeed, my lord."

"I do as well. Very much so, in fact," he said, offering her a wide smile. "I don't believe we have been introduced."

She schooled her features, hoping he didn't notice the inevitable blush of her cheeks. "We haven't, but I won't tell anyone if you won't."

He laughed, and the sound of it was almost enough to make her flutter her lashes, which was ridiculous.

"I'm Viscount Callan, my lady." He gave her a small bow and winked when he stood.

The man was an obvious flirt, but given that no man had ever deigned to flirt with her, she could see how it was indeed effective.

"Lady Lily," she responded.

Realization washed over his face. "Ah, you are being courted by Lord Knox, I hear."

She wasn't sure why his words irked her as much as they did. He wasn't wrong, she supposed, but she didn't like him viewing her as attached to another man. Not that she would ever be anything to Lord Callan, so it didn't matter, but it ground at her nerves, regardless.

"We're getting to know each other. I just met him tonight," she replied. It was the truth, and for some reason, she didn't wish to speak the words of courtship.

"Surely he won't mind if I ask you about the plays you have seen? I'd love to hear your perspective."

If a man could grow even more attractive before a woman's eyes, Viscount Callan had just done so, and knowing he would never see her the same way may just be the greatest tragedy she could imagine for her life.

Chapter 3

Alexander Bourke, Viscount Callan, was utterly intrigued by the charming Lady Lily. He typically avoided marriage-minded misses, but there was something different about her. She wasn't like any of the other women in attendance. It wasn't just that she was different in appearance, although he found her to be quite pretty, beautiful if he were honest, but it was in how she carried herself.

She didn't try to win the favor of anyone or capture the attention of the room. The few freckles on her nose and cheeks added to her charm, and he glanced at them when she spoke. He could tell by the way her light blue eyes moved behind her rounded spectacles she was a person who remained constantly in thought. He had always found intelligence and meaningful conversation appealing but often lacking among the shallow members of the society they both circulated in.

"Before the house party, Rosina…I mean, Lady Preston, and I went to see *A Love For a Lady*, and it was wonderful. I am not one often brought to tears, but I admit my eyes did not remain dry during the performance."

Alex didn't find it hard to believe that she wasn't the type to go into hysterics. She seemed far too reserved and controlled for such behavior, even if he had just met her. "What was it you enjoyed most about it?"

"Stormy Wells has a way of capturing human emotions in his words, and the actors were superb as well, of course. The depth of the heroine and her heartbreak, and the healing that she encountered on her path to love. It was just so…real. I could feel it."

He noticed something changed in her expression, something almost painful.

"Does that resonate with you, my lady? Have you had your heart broken?" The notion irritated him, and for some reason, he hated the thought of some cad doing so. He knew far too well what it felt like.

She narrowed her eyes at him. "It's forward of you to ask, my lord, but no, not in the way you mean. The heart can be broken for a multitude of reasons."

Something about her made him long to know more about her. And call it his sense of honor, but he didn't like the tiniest thought that someone could have hurt someone as charming as her.

"Will you tell me about it?" he asked.

She looked at him as if he had gone mad, and he supposed he had. He was being far too forward, and she had every right to tell him to bugger off. He enjoyed experiencing and learning about the experiences of others since it aided and inspired him with his writing.

"Why would you care to know, my lord?"

He shifted on his feet. Alex didn't have a suitable answer for that. Not one that he would share with her, anyway. He fought to find the right words to respond to her with.

"I'm just curious. My gentlemanly principles got the better of me at the thought of anyone having distressed you."

"I don't need saving, Lord Callan. But I appreciate the sentiment," she replied. He knew she was going to turn things around on him when her eyebrow arched. "Would you like to tell me about the heartbreak you have endured?"

No. Never. Not in the slightest. If he could go his entire life without recalling the lowest point of his life—he would pay a king's ransom to ensure it. "I see your point, my lady. Please accept my apologies for asking."

Her expression shifted back to a sweet smile, and the tension left his body. For some reason, he dreaded the thought of her harboring the slightest irritation towards him.

"You are forgiven." She widened her smile.

She really was quite beautiful. He was almost certain she didn't realize it, which made her even more so. Lord Knox was going to be a lucky man to win her hand.

"Lily, are you ready to retire for the evening? I was going to head up," a woman's voice said.

Alex shook off his thoughts about Lady Lily and noted that Lady Preston had joined them.

"Yes, I shall walk up with you." She shifted her attention back to Alex. "I'm sure we will speak more soon."

"I look forward to it," he replied. He watched her walk away with her friend, and there wasn't a bit of falsehood or pretense in his words. He would certainly look forward to speaking with her again.

Alex took the opportunity to retire to his chamber for the evening as well. Once his valet had helped him ready himself for bed and departed, Alex sat in a chair by the fire with his writing journal. He dipped his quill in the ink sitting on the table beside him and jotted several of his thoughts from the day.

He smiled, recalling everything about Lady Lily. She would make the perfect heroine in a play. He didn't want to forget any detail about her or their conversation, so he wrote until he captured it all. Her hair, her quick wit, and everything about her form.

By the time he finished writing, he noticed his cock pained from straining against his breeches, the only clothing he wore beneath his banyan. He groaned and forced himself to shake off the reaction. He was a man, and it had been a bit since he'd been with a woman, so he told himself that it meant nothing. Well, it meant that perhaps he needed to wet his wick soon since it had been a while, but nothing besides that.

The next morning, Alex strolled into the breakfast room to join the other guests. He glanced at the long table as he made his way to the sideboard and noticed Lady Lily sitting with Knox. It annoyed him slightly but only because he would have enjoyed speaking with her. For no other reason than that. She was interesting and intelligent, which made conversation with her easy.

He made his selections, filling his plate before he found a seat across from where the couple sat, but a few guests down. He was close enough that he could see them, but not close enough to join in their conversation. It was probably for the best. If the man was courting her, he shouldn't take up her time just because he found her to be a stimulating conversationalist.

Alex speared a bite of his eggs and brought the fork to his mouth, watching Lady Lily's lips move. He couldn't help but wonder what she was speaking to Lord Knox about. From the delight in her expression, she seemed to enjoy herself. He continued eating while he watched them. It nagged at him, and then, when he glanced at Knox, it gnawed at his insides even more. It was clear the man was politely tolerating her company at best. He wasn't rude or ignoring her, but his smile didn't reach his eyes. He didn't appreciate the conversation, and that seemed like a shame to Alex.

Once his plate was empty, he realized he hadn't spoken to anyone for the entire breakfast and had just watched Lady Lily, willing the roar of the surrounding conversations to quiet down enough that he might hear the things she spoke about.

Before he had time to think more about that insight, their hostess encouraged them all outside for a game of Pall Mall, organized into partners. He noticed Knox remained to the side with some of the other guests who intended to be spectators for the event, and that meant he wouldn't partner with Lady Lily. He watched her for a moment as the other players sought their partners and she stood waiting to see if anyone would ask her.

Alex noted the disappointment in her expression, and it pained him more than he cared to admit. Alex rushed to her, moving through the other guests.

"Would you partner with me, my lady?"

She looked up at him and grinned. "I would be delighted, my lord."

"Why don't you select a mallet for us?"

She moved to the rack and selected the blue one, holding it up to him as if she were asking for his approval.

He nodded, and she returned to his side. "I must warn you, my lord, that I am not very good at this game."

"Well, we are well matched because I am unlikely to hit the ball straight even once." It was true. He was never one to have the patience to master such games, but it never bothered him to admit defeat. At least in the matter of yard games.

"Well, that takes the pressure off, then," she said. "We shall pass the morning without the spirited competition."

They lined up with the others and would take their turn last. With the way the hostess organized the game, each team would share a ball and mallet and would take turns hitting the ball when it was their turn again. The first team to get their ball through the last wicket would win a prize.

Once their turn came around, Alex let Lady Lily take the first swing, which sent them close to a large tree. They moved together to wait by their ball for their next turn.

Alex didn't mind that they were a bit separated from the other guests, if only so that he might converse with her without worrying that others might interfere with their conversation.

"Tell me something no one else knows about you," he said, deciding he didn't wish to waste time with all the polite pleasantries about the weather and how kind their hosts were.

If he expected her to drop her mouth open in shock from his statement, he would be disappointed. "Well, that shouldn't be a challenge, since I don't have all that many friends."

He noticed she didn't seem upset by her statement, and he found her comfort with who she was intriguing.

"Well, tell me something anyway."

She thought for a moment and bit into her bottom lip. The action made him notice her lips again and how full they were, and he drew a deep breath when she began speaking again, if only to give him something else to focus on. "I speak six different languages."

"That is quite impressive," he said, in genuine awe of her abilities. "I assume French is one of them?"

"Oui, monsieur."

"I happen to be proficient in that particular language. What do you say we only speak in French for the rest of the game?" he asked, then chastised himself for not stating his idea in French, which would have impressed her far more.

But the smile she gave him at the suggestion made him quickly forget his error.

"Vous revenez," she said, motioning to the ball when it was his turn again.

"Merci." He took his swing and missed the wicket. They both laughed and started after the ball so they could await their next turn.

As the morning progressed, he found it to be one of the most enjoyable encounters he'd had in a long time. The conversation was engaging, and her French was excellent. He learnt more about the books she read and that she enjoyed doing maths in her head and reciting entire plays to cope with mundane social events. He found her ability to memorize plays fascinating.

Alex rarely spoke much about himself to anyone, but he opened up to Lady Lily. He told her a bit about what he enjoyed studying at university, as well as a little about his family, especially his younger siblings, who were quite the handful. He learnt she also had a younger brother, who was away at Eton for school.

Neither one of them spoke a word of English for the rest of the game until Lord Irvine and Lady Eliza were finally declared the winners.

"That was fun, my lady," Alex said, returning to English. "We shall have to do that again sometime. I may have to become proficient in Italian next."

"If you do, I shall be happy to help you practice."

He looked at her, and their gazes held for several moments. Forcing himself to look away, he glanced across the grass at the other guests. "Should I return you to Knox?" he asked.

She also looked at the other guests. "I don't see him anywhere."

For a man who was supposed to be courting the lady, he didn't seem to put much effort into keeping her attention for himself. Alex couldn't decide why that annoyed and delighted him so much.

"There is Rosina," she said. "I believe I shall join her for a while."

Alex extended his arm to her. "Allow me to escort you to her."

She took his arm, and they moved at a leisurely pace until they reached her friend.

"If you will excuse me, I shall see you both later," Alex said, bowing to them.

He had the urge to remove himself from her presence. There was something about her that made him think and feel things he wasn't certain he wished to feel. And certainly not for a woman who was being courted by an earl, one of his fellow peers at the same house party.

Alex decided he would return to his room for the afternoon and write. He had many thoughts and happenings from the day that he wished to get out of his head and onto parchment. The way his writings were coming together, Lady Lily might just be the basis for one of his next plays. One of the wildly popular Stormy Wells plays the whole of society had no idea was written by a viscount of the *ton*. It was his best-kept secret and one he would never divulge if he could help it.

Focusing on his parchment, Alex would spend the afternoon buried in his writings and just might succeed at convincing himself that as intriguing as she was, and what a great story her character could tell, he felt nothing deeper for Lady Lily.

Chapter 4

The next day, Lily struggled with her muddled thoughts. She wasn't certain what she wanted anymore. She had resigned herself to be a spinster who would enjoy attending the theatre and reading all the latest books, perhaps hearing about Rosina's latest conquests. Assuming her friend remained resolved in her desire to remain an unmarried widow. She would have been perfectly at ease and content with such a life. Then somehow her life became far more complicated than all that.

There was Lord Knox, who was a mystery in his own right. He didn't seem ready to profess any kind of love or adoration for her. Far from it, in fact. Nor did he befit a man who was teetering towards a proposal, but he had a kind warmth to him. He sought her out the previous afternoon and spent a few hours by her side after the Pall Mall tournament, although she noticed he was still distracted at times. Lord Knox admitted to her he wasn't good at such matters of courtship, and she could appreciate his honesty. Besides, neither was she.

She was almost certain she would feel nothing for the man beyond friendship, but that wouldn't matter in the least to her father. Her determined father had his own expectations, and he was also the one who held all the control over her life. If she had to marry Lord Knox, she was at least fairly certain he would never harm her and would allow her to live a life close to the one she had imagined for herself. She didn't picture him as a passionate husband, or even one attentive enough to involve himself with her interests beyond casual conversation.

In some ways, she thought such a match could be perfect for her. She would be out from under her father's control and would be able to mostly do what she pleased with an agreeable husband. She had never thought that love, or passion, or even attraction would be part of her future, and never thought to hope for such things.

But then Lord Callan had made his way into her sphere, and he became quite difficult to dislodge from her every thought. She had never felt more seen by another person than she did in his presence. She wasn't aware of the power of such a revelation, and it only pulled her in further when she noticed how he gazed at her. No one in her entire life had truly seen her before. Perhaps Rosina, but that wasn't the same. She wasn't seen for her intelligence, her personality, and certainly not her appearance. The perpetual wallflower in her own life, and yet the most intriguing man she had ever met appeared to have taken notice of her.

She very well could have imagined all of it. It could have been a foolish girl's wishful thinking, misreading the man's polite, good-natured intentions. To think that the wallflower of the *ton* would attract one of the most handsome men was something that would happen in one of her beloved plays, but certainly not in real life.

Lily chastised herself for only thinking about his appearance. Doing so was shallow and didn't do him justice. That was the real tragedy of the matter. He was far more than just handsome. He was witty, clever, intelligent, and passionate. She blushed thinking about him as being passionate, but she imagined he was quite experienced in all the things that occurred between a woman and a man that Rosina had told her about.

"Are you all right, my lady?" Lord Knox asked from beside her.

She refocused her attention on her horse. After they broke their fast that morning, a riding group organized to tour the estate before they would enjoy a picnic by the pond. She hadn't ridden since before the season began, so it would be in her best interest to cease with the woolgathering and focus on controlling her mare.

"Indeed," she replied. "Just getting comfortable in the saddle again."

Lord Demming approached, traveling in the opposite direction, catching Lord Knox's attention. "I forgot I have to get a missive out straight away. Would you be willing to come back with me and then we'll catch up to the group?"

"Of course, my lord," Lord Knox replied. He looked over at her and gave her a small smile and a nod. And she waved him off.

At least she wouldn't have to attempt conversation with him when her mind was muddled, which wasn't a state she had ever been accustomed to.

"Lady Lily," that intoxicating rich baritone called out from beside her. She hadn't even noticed he had caught up to her.

"Lord Callan." She wasn't typically at a loss for words, just a loss for someone to speak the words to, but for the first time, she struggled to find something to say.

"I saw Knox returned to the stables, so I thought you could use a bit of company."

"That would be appreciated, thank you."

Lily wanted to roll her eyes at how high her voice became when she responded. She wasn't sure she sounded like herself—more like a simpering miss than that of her own voice. Lily drew a deep breath, steadying herself. Perhaps she could make him do most of the talking this time.

She glanced over at him and found him looking back at her, then shifted her gaze back to the front. "Why don't you tell me something no one knows about you?" she asked.

He remained quiet, so she glanced at him again, finding him in thought as if he warred with what he wished to disclose. She watched him, eager to learn what he might share about himself.

"I write," he finally said.

She wasn't sure what she expected him to say, but she didn't think it was that.

"What do you write?"

"All manner of things. Journal entries, short stories, poems, even tried my hand at a few plays."

She turned her head to look at him again. He seemed nervous to share such personal information about himself, and it endeared him to her even more than he already was.

"That explains why you asked me about what I enjoyed most in the plays I've seen. I am impressed, my lord. I would love to read some of your stories or works some-time."

A smile played at the corners of his lips. "I'll think about it."

"Do you not wish for anyone to know about your writing? I would think it was such a thing others would know about you."

He glanced forward and drew a breath. She allowed her gaze to glance lower and noticed how his thigh appeared even more taut, and she swallowed hard. What was it about his thighs that she couldn't stop looking? When she had never noticed them at all on a man before Lord Callan.

"I have told no one that secret about myself before. My writing is for me, a way to express myself with anything that I might be feeling at the moment."

"I believe I may be the opposite," she replied.

"What do you mean?"

"That is what reading and the theatre are for me. I lose myself in books and plays because I relate to the emotion and angst of the characters. Perhaps I even live vicariously through them at times." She regretted the words as soon as they left her lips. What happened to letting him do more of the talking and not adding to her muddled thoughts?

She kept her gaze forward, not wanting to meet his eye, or to know if he stared at her, or worse, pitied her.

"I understand," he said. "I do the same with characters I write."

"I wouldn't think a handsome viscount would have much need to escape his life," she said, knowing she was being far too bold, but each of their positions in life was not the same.

"So you think I'm handsome?"

Lily looked at him again, this time so he could see how she rolled her eyes. "You know you are. And wealthy, and titled, and a man. From my vantage point, it would appear you don't have all that much to live through others to achieve."

His brow furrowed as if she struck a nerve. "If we go by your logic, neither do you. Unless you wish to be a man, that is. Because, from everything I see before me, you are indeed a woman with a titled father, and a beautiful one at that."

"Don't say things you don't mean, my lord." She didn't want fake compliments and pretense between them. It was wholly unnecessary and did nothing to change who she was.

"Which part? That you are a woman? Please forgive me if I was incorrect on that point," he said, giving her a wolfish grin, and it did things to her insides.

"You know which part," she replied, looking back forward. "No one has ever thought of me as beautiful. My own mama would balk at such a statement."

"Then perhaps your mama should be horsewhipped."

Her head shot in his direction. "My lord!"

He met her gaze, and she couldn't look away from the hold his intense green eyes had on her. "I will speak plainly so that perhaps you will hear me this time. You are among the most beautiful of women. These other chits don't hold a candle to you, and I won't have you, or anyone else, saying otherwise."

Lily swallowed hard, and all words and coherent thought left her head. She looked back at the path and fought to get control over her mind and body. She tensed and delighted at his words. The way he spoke, she knew he meant what he said, or at least believed he did, but it did nothing to assuage her growing attachment to the man, which wasn't ideal.

They arrived at the location for the picnic before they could speak anything else to each other. He climbed down from his horse. Before she could do so herself, he was in front of her and his hands were on her hips, lifting her down.

The feel of his large, powerful hands on her sent electric pulses throughout her entire body. She had never experienced such a sensation before, and when he released his hands, her skin grew cold from the loss of his touch. She looked up at him, and her heart flipped from the soft smile he gave her.

"May I escort you?" he asked, shifting to stand beside her and extending his arm.

She tucked her hand in the crook, and the electricity returned when she gripped his muscular forearm.

There were five blankets already set out, with baskets in the middle of each one. Lord Callan led her to the furthest blanket from the other guests and helped her to seat herself before settling beside her. But not as close to her person as she'd prefer, if she were being honest. She had to remind herself that they were in full view of the other guests, and besides, he would not marry her, even if he found her to be as beautiful as he said.

He prepared her a plate from the selections in the basket. She took the plate but didn't meet his eye, keeping her chin down as she stared at the chicken, cheese, and fruit on her plate.

"Did I say something to upset you, my lady?"

"Not at all. It's just…"

He glanced around to ensure no one was in earshot. "It's just what? You can tell me."

"I should have thanked you for your compliment. I apologize for the lack of manners. I am just not used to receiving them. So I guess what I am saying is thank you, my lord."

"That is the fault of these idiots, and not one of your own doing. You need not apologize for their shortcomings," he replied, all seriousness in his tone and not a single hit of pity, which she appreciated.

They fell into a prolonged silence again. Surprisingly, it wasn't awkward. She glanced at him, just as he did the same, their gazes holding for a few seconds.

Lord Callan cleared his throat and glanced at his plate. "I didn't ask where Lord Knox went. Was he going to rejoin the group?"

"He went back with Lord Demming, but I believe they were going to join everyone." She glanced around and didn't see him anywhere. If she were honest, his disappearance had not disappointed her. It gave her more time with Lord Callan, to whom she feared she could easily lose her heart if she wasn't careful.

"I am grateful that you have allowed me to keep you company in his absence."

"I enjoy your company," she said before taking a bite of a piece of chicken.

The lopsided grin he gave her almost caused her to choke on the bite, but she quickly recovered.

"I very much enjoy spending time with you," he replied.

She wasn't certain where it came from, but a streak of boldness coursed through her. "Why have you never married, my lord?"

Chapter 5

L ily wasn't even certain she wished to know the answer. The man could have a mistress he was in love with. He could prefer the company of men, something she had been intrigued to learn about from Rosina. But he appeared to her to be around six or seven-and-twenty, and of an age to have taken a wife.

He appeared taken aback by her question and opened his mouth to speak before closing it again.

"Forgive me," she blurted. "I shouldn't have asked."

"There is nothing to forgive," he said, his tone soft. "It's just that I don't trust all that easily. And that is all I shall share at present."

She wondered what happened to him, or what someone had done to him to break his trust. Her heart pained for him, and she longed to brush his hair back from his forehead and cup his chiseled cheek.

Before she could give in to something so forward and scandalous, two horses galloped towards the group and slowed to a stop. Lord Knox hopped down from one of them and scanned the guests until he caught her gaze. He started straight to her, and she was a bit saddened by his reappearance and knowing she wouldn't be able to continue speaking with Lord Callan as they had been.

"I do hope you will accept my apologies. It was a lucky thing that I had accompanied Lord Demming as we got turned around on the way to rejoin everyone," Lord Knox said.

"That is quite all right, my lord. Lord Callan was kind enough to keep me company."

Lord Knox gave Lord Callan a polite nod of thanks.

The gentleman spoke back and forth to each other about something, but she didn't hear it. She let her thoughts drift to the reaction she had to Lord Callan and to all he had shared. She wasn't even certain the man considered her in the same way she did him. He could find her to be a beautiful woman and not want anything more than friendship. Men believed their mothers and sisters to be beautiful, too, so the words didn't signify.

If Lord Knox offered for her, that was who her father was going to accept—if he hadn't already—and that was that. It wouldn't do her any good to imagine otherwise.

She attempted to refocus herself on the conversation and she noticed Lord Callan casting her a curious glance.

Nearby, the other guests readied themselves to head back to the stables. The clouds had rolled in, and the sky had grown darker. It appeared that they may all get caught in the rain if they didn't make haste to depart.

Lord Knox rose and then reached out to her to help her stand. It was painfully obvious that she didn't have the same reaction to the man as she had to Lord Callan. She wasn't certain if it would have made things better or more complicated if she had. She decided on the former. As if she reacted to both, she could at least tell herself that she would lead a contended life if she ended up married to Lord Knox, which was almost certain to be her future.

She slipped her hand into the crook of Lord Knox's arm and glanced back at Lord Callan to see him following behind them. Lord Knox led her to their horses and helped her into her sidesaddle. He leapt onto his own horse and continued on with the group, so she followed behind.

Lord Callan caught up to her and was at her side in a matter of moments.

They trotted along in silence until a crack of lightning, followed by a crash of thunder, made her jump in the saddle. She recovered and kept herself from losing her seat.

"We must quicken our pace," Lord Callan called out beside her. She glanced back, and Lady Juliet was far off in the distance with Lord Camden.

"Should we help them?" Lady Lily asked.

"We are better off sending someone back. I believe the lady's horse is afraid of the impending storm. Camden is looking after her."

The rain fell harder and had reached her cheeks. Lily urged her horse into a gallop, intending to get back to the open field as quickly as possible so they could race across the grass to the stables.

She glanced over her shoulder and saw Lord Callan following behind her. They cleared the trees, and he caught up to her, galloping at her side across the field. The other guests were ahead of them on the other side of the field, also racing to get out of the rain.

Suddenly, the clouds erupted, and the rain fell hard and fast. In a matter of moments, Lily became soaked, and the rain only kept coming down in buckets. The wind took her riding hat, and it blew away, but she didn't slow her pace. Lord Callan glanced back, and she waved forward, indicating she didn't wish for him to go back for her hat.

Lily shivered from the cold but pressed on. The galloping loosened the pins in her hair until they fell out, releasing her coiffure so that her long tresses fell down her back as she rode.

They finally reached the stables and were under cover from the rain. Many other guests had dismounted and were making their way inside. Lord Camden and Lady Juliet came riding in with her straddling the gentleman. Lily pretended not to take notice of the improper position they were in.

A groom started in her direction, but Lord Callan had jumped down and was at her side before the groom could assist.

"We must get you inside. You are surely almost frozen," he said, lifting her down from the saddle.

He took her hand in his, and even through their wet gloves, she already felt warmer. Hastening their steps, they hurried towards the house. Lord Callan opened the door and allowed her to enter first, then followed her.

She waited for him, and they fell in step beside each other. "I must look like a dreadful mess," she said, stopping to take off her spectacles and do her best to dry them.

Lord Callan stopped with her and dug out his handkerchief. "Try this. It feels dry enough." He handed it to her, and she noticed his gaze appeared to linger on her, from what she could tell with her limited eyesight. "You are…breathtaking," he whispered.

"My lord?" She slid her glasses back on her face, and he took another step closer to her.

"And now you are perfect."

Her lips parted from gasping at his words. She wasn't sure if she had heard him correctly, but he stood before her, staring at her as if she were the most precious thing in the world. It had to be a dream, as it wasn't possible that he looked at her that way. His eyes darted to her lips, and the attention there made her bite one side of her bottom lip.

He looked around, then pulled her into an alcove that was just behind where he stood. Her heart raced with anticipation at what he might do, knowing she wanted whatever it might be. He removed his glove and cupped her right cheek with his bare hand, turning them so he hid her body with his own.

"I'm going to kiss you now."

She could only nod in response, her body instinctively leaning closer to him.

He leaned forward and softly pressed his lips to hers, feathering a few light kisses. She sighed, resting her gloved hands on his firm chest. She had the strongest urge to massage the muscles beneath her fingers, but before she could decide if she would do so, he wrapped his arms around her and kissed her again. When he ran his tongue along the seam of her lips, she opened to him, and he swept his tongue into her mouth.

The taste of the wine he drank at the picnic and the velvety feel of his tongue massaging hers caused the place between her legs to throb with need. He didn't relent, and she released a low mewl when he lightly sucked her tongue into his mouth and then massaged it with his again. Even soaked from the rain, she knew there was heat and dampness between her thighs that was for him.

He broke their kiss and kissed along her jaw and then her neck. Every bit of her skin tingled and heated from the places he touched with his lips and tongue.

"My lord," she whispered.

He stopped and stared into her eyes, and even in the dark alcove, she could see the depth of his desire in them. "Alex."

"Alex," she whispered, not looking away.

He dipped his head to kiss her neck again, sliding one of his hands from her back across her rib cage and up to her breast, which she had never realized how much she longed for attention there. He lifted her breast and massaged it in his hand, which caused her to release a series of low moans.

Alex kissed higher on her neck until he reached her ear and whispered against it, "Did you like that?"

She nodded.

His fingers shifted to dance across the top of her breast before he dipped his hand below her neckline and lifted her breast from her wet stays. Her damp skin exposed to the cold air caused her to shiver. She gripped the lapels of his coat, steading herself.

He leaned his head down and flicked her nipple with his tongue before sucking it into his mouth. Her head rolled back, and she arched her back, pressing her chest harder against his mouth. She felt him smile against her breast before he lifted the other one and repeated the attention with his mouth to her other nipple.

"Alex," she moaned. She shivered again, and he stopped what he was doing.

He stared at her, attempting to catch his own breath. "I got carried away," he said, tucking her breasts back into her gown.

"I enjoyed it very much," she whispered, her hands still holding on to his coat.

He leaned down and kissed her one more time. "You are soaked and need dry clothes before you catch a cold." He rubbed along her arms as if to warm her.

She released the hold she had on his coat, even though every part of her body longed to pull him closer instead. She had the urge to rub the place that ached against him, to soothe the need that built within her.

He slipped his glove back on his hand, then turned and peeked his head out of the alcove. Grabbing her hand, he pulled her back into the hallway. "You must change right away. I hope there is a fire in your chamber."

She noted he didn't release her hand, and she had no inclination to pull it away from him. Lily allowed him to lead her to the main staircase.

Her heart raced just as hard as when he had kissed her, the electricity from his gloved touch still enough to make her rethink everything she thought she knew. Was that the feeling she had read about in her books and watched in her plays? The passion that drives one to such distraction that they would risk everything if it meant they could receive just one more kiss. Just one more touch. Just one more anything, as long as it was Alex who gave it.

Lily glanced over at him as they climbed the stairs, and he looked as if he were pondering something. She couldn't make out his expression, but she thought she saw a bit of confusion in his furrowed brow.

"Alex?"

He shook off his thoughts and looked at her when they reached the top of the staircase.

"I'll see you at dinner," he said, bowing to her, then departing to the wing where most of the gentlemen were staying.

She hurried to her room and was relieved to find her maid, Posy, waiting for her. Posy helped her out of her wet clothing, and she donned her dressing robe to sit before the fire. Lily stared into the flames, attempting to make sense of the thoughts garbled in her head.

Bringing her fingers to her lips, she touched where he had kissed her. She closed her eyes and relived every detail, the heat building in her core again. It might be the most wicked she had ever been, and she might end up married to another man, but more than anything, she wanted to kiss Alex again. And so much more, not that she could admit such a thing to anyone, ever.

Chapter 6

Alex was still on edge from when he had kissed Lily the day before. She hadn't given him leave to refer to her by her given name, but in his dreams when she came to him, he thought of her as his Lily. Alex kept his distance from her the evening after their kiss, with Lord Knox in her presence. He wasn't certain of the state of the man's courtship, and he didn't wish to interfere.

He supposed that wasn't exactly true. If one didn't wish to interfere, they shouldn't do the things he did to the lady in an alcove. If she hadn't shivered from being in soaked clothing, he couldn't swear that he might not have done more. She had been a goddess with her long red hair down around her waist and her eyelids heavy from desire.

He wasn't the type of man who dallied with innocents, but there was something about her. Lily drew him in. She was like a perfect rose, just beginning to bloom. She didn't even realize it, which made her even more tempting and beautiful.

It wasn't in his imagination how she responded to him. Hell, she said she enjoyed it. But then she was seated with Knox at dinner, and he was in her presence most of the evening. She didn't seem all that interested in the man, and every time he glanced at her, her gaze found its way to his.

But he had believed that before, and the lady chose the other gentleman, he reminded himself. The pain of that realization hit him harder than he cared to admit. He tried to shake it off, but the pain of those scars coming to the surface told him to guard his heart from bringing the same torture and misery upon himself yet again.

Once he dressed that next morning, he made his way to the breakfast room. Lily was seated at the table by herself, so he quickly made his selections and took the seat beside her.

"Did you enjoy the music last night?" he asked.

"Very much so. Did you?"

He took a bite of his eggs and swallowed before answering. "I did. I was surprised you didn't perform."

She released a stream of laughter, and he grinned at the way it sounded like the most beautiful, melodic bells. "You never want to hear me sing. I never had much talent for music."

"Well, I am far more impressed with your skills in maths and languages anyway," he said, winking at her.

He glanced over at her after he took a bite of toast, and her cheeks were a pretty shade of pink. He pushed aside the thoughts of what color her skin would be if he did all the things he dreamt of the previous evening. His cock twitched, already far too aware of her presence.

"Are you going on the trip to the village today?" he asked.

"I am," she replied, glancing around the room as if she were looking for someone. "Lord Knox is supposed to escort me."

She shifted her focus back to Alex. "Would you join us?"

The last thing Alex wished to do was to be the third wheel to whatever the situation was between her and Knox. It was all too familiar and reminded him he was quickly losing control of the situation between them.

"I believe I am going to stay back today." He leaned closer and lowered his voice. "I have some writing to do."

She grinned at him, and the air threatened to leave his body at how much he wished to pick her up and carry her from the room. The characters in the play he was writing would do just that. If he couldn't do and say the things he wished to her in real life, he certainly could in his play.

After breakfast, Alex spent hours poring over his writing. He continued to work on the idea for his next play and wanted to get as much as he could down on paper. It hadn't been as easy as he had hoped to make progress since his thoughts kept shifting to Lily and what she was doing at the village with Knox. The thought only made him want to break his quill and throw it across the room. A childish action, to be sure, but he kept enough control over his ire to keep his quill intact and pressed to the parchment. He did his best to push it aside and use his irritation as motivation and ideas for his writing.

It hadn't been easy keeping his writing a secret. His father would find such a thing to be a waste of time. He would tell Alex that it was time he could spend managing his estates and partaking in activities that would be deemed more accepted by society. His father might suffer apoplexy if he knew Alex sold his plays, as earning an income from such an effort would be deemed an act beneath the members of their society.

The haute ton enjoyed having money, but they didn't work or dirty their hands with the actions required to make money besides participating in society and coordinating with their men of business.

So he wrote in secret and did what he wished, with no one being the wiser. His encounter with the enticing Lady Lily had inspired him. Everything about her had driven him to distraction, and he feared he was steadily losing his heart to her. He wasn't certain he would survive another heartbreak after he picked up the pieces from the last one, especially given that he had never felt as strong a feeling for anyone as he did for Lily.

Lily wasn't just beautiful. She was the type of woman who would challenge him intellectually. She shared the same interests he did, possibly more so. He had never been compelled to share his biggest secret with anyone, but yet he was already tempted to do so with her.

Alex hadn't been opposed to marriage, the opposite, in fact, until he had experienced the sting of rejection. Marrying just any chit in order to get an heir off of her didn't sit right with him. There was a part of him concerned a wife might not appreciate the time he spent writing, but he believed Lily would find his writing intriguing. That she would be proud of him.

A wide grin formed at the thought of her reading over his work and giving him her input. He also thought about what it would be like to have her at his side every day and in his bed every night, which he quickly came to realize that he wanted more than anything.

Tossing his quill on the desk in his chamber, Alex decided he was far too distracted to get any more writing done that day. He rose and stretched his arms wide after he had remained seated for so long. Alex decided he would see if perhaps the guests had returned from the village, and if not, he would take a walk and think about what he wished to do about his growing feelings for Lily.

She may come back betrothed to Knox, and then there would be nothing he could do. Knots formed in his stomach at the thought that she would be lost to him. He wasn't certain he could allow that to happen, but that would mean he must offer for her. Especially if her father was so intent on seeing her wed to a titled gentleman. What if she didn't accept him? She seemed as affected by their kiss as he was.

Alex made his way downstairs, finding many guests congregating in the salon and on the terrace. He glanced around for Lily and didn't see her anywhere. He continued on to the terrace and took the stairs down to the yard, intending to clear his mind with a bit of fresh air.

Once he reached the back of the house, he noted Lily following Lord Camden around to the other side of the house. Camden glanced around as if he were determining if they had been seen, and Alex backed out of sight.

What was she doing sneaking out with the man? Marquess Theodore Camden was a notorious rake of the *ton* and could only attempt to lure Lily away from the other guests for nefarious reasons. Especially since he had spent most of the house party with Lady Juliet.

After a few moments, Alex moved again, hurrying in the direction they had gone. Bile rose in his throat, thinking about why a known rake would pursue the woman he loved. He loved her? He shook off the thought, unwilling to allow himself to ponder his feelings at present. First, he needed to ensure that the blackguard didn't put a single finger on Lily.

He peeked around the corner when he reached the side of the house they had disappeared to. Alex wasn't quite certain he could believe what he saw. Lily leaned against the brick of the house, looking at where Camden sat on the grass with charcoals and parchment. He appeared to be drawing her. Why would the man do so?

Alex couldn't help but watch them. They didn't even speak to each other. Camden looked up every so often from his parchment and then back to continue his work.

He must have watched them for at least a half hour before Camden said something to her.

He held his breath, hoping he might hear what they said. Unable to make out the words, he only heard low mumbles. Lily started in his direction, but Camden remained behind. Alex jumped behind a bush, hiding himself so she didn't see him.

Lily passed by and returned the way she came. He listened to see if Camden would follow, but he hadn't done so yet. The bush rustled as Alex worked his way out once he was certain Lily was out of sight. He went to round the corner and walked straight into Camden.

"Callan," the man said, taking a few steps back with wide eyes. "What are you doing out here?"

"I could ask you the same thing."

The man gave him an indifferent shrug, and Alex clenched his jaw.

"Just out for a walk."

Liar. The man would tell Alex what he was about, even if it required physical means to do so.

"Then why did I see Lady Lily out here with you? Surely, with your reputation, you don't expect me to believe that you had innocent intentions."

Camden sighed and waved him off. "She agreed to help me with something. We became friends of sorts during our trip to the village. Nothing more, I assure you."

"I thought Knox was her escort to the village."

Camden eyed him curiously. "He wasn't feeling well, or I believe that is what Lady Lily said."

Alex rubbed his hand down his face. He could have spent the day with her instead of allowing the rake before him to do so.

"What did you need her help with?"

"Why do you care so much? If you have your sights set on the lady, I assure you I do not have a horse in that particular race."

"Just answer the question," Alex ground out. "What were you doing with her, away from the rest of the guests? You appeared to be drawing something."

It was Camden's turn to clench his jaw. "I shall show you, but you will keep this to yourself."

Alex nodded in agreement.

The man pulled the parchment from a satchel he carried and handed it to Alex.

Alex's breath caught at what he saw. Camden had drawn her and captured her with the precision of a professional artist. She was almost just as beautiful on paper as she was in person. From one artist of sorts to another, Alex was impressed with the man's talent.

He glanced up at Camden. "Why? Why did you draw this?"

"She has such a unique beauty, and I wanted to see if I could capture her essence on parchment. The rest is my business, and I ask you to pretend you saw nothing. I don't have designs on Lady Lily if that is what you are concerned about."

Alex released a sigh of relief and stared at the drawing again. "Can I keep this?" Alex asked. "I'll pay you for it."

Camden gave him a knowing grin, and it annoyed Alex to no end. "It's all yours. I wish you luck with the lady."

The man stepped around him and took off around the side of the house before Alex could say anything else. He stared down at the drawing again. He closed his eyes, allowing himself to accept what he already suspected to be true. Alex was in love with Lily, and he couldn't handle another heartbreak.

Chapter 7

Alex had searched for Lily after his encounter with Camden, but when he didn't see her anywhere, he assumed she must have returned to her chamber. He did the same so he could put the drawing in a safe place instead of tucked inside the breast pocket of his coat.

Once he had returned to join the rest of the party for dinner, he watched Lily in the company of Knox. The man didn't leave her side the entire time, listening as she spoke to him. Alex tried to determine what topics they might speak about, but he couldn't hear them or make out what she was saying. If only he could determine if she was interested in the man. He wouldn't have thought so by the way she had encouraged Alex's kiss, but she could have only been caught up in the moment.

At dinner, he was seated away from them, so he didn't get a chance to engage her then either. He glanced at her, hoping she might glance in his direction, but she spent most of the meal in animated conversation, seemingly enjoying herself.

He tamped down his jealousy and irritation. After dinner was over and the gentlemen rejoined the ladies in the salon, their hostess suggested a game of charades. Alex fought not to roll his eyes. As a playwright, he enjoyed charades and the practice of expressing ideas through acting and dramatics, but if he didn't speak with Lily, he might explode. He wasn't sure what she thought after their kiss, or more importantly, if she intended to wed Knox.

Alex tried to focus his attention on the game, but he kept glancing out of the corner of his eye where Lily sat on a settee with Knox at her side. The man didn't appear besotted with her, or even overly interested, but he stayed by her side all evening. Perhaps he should ask the man what his intentions were and then determine what he would do to win her once he knew if Knox would remain a competition for him.

After the game had ended, they rose and Knox bowed to her, taking his leave to exit the salon. Alex didn't waste a moment and appeared at her side.

"Follow me," he said to Lily. He hadn't planned out where he would lead her or what he might even say, but he had to take the only opportunity he had to get her alone.

She followed Alex across the salon, and they exited out to the terrace. He closed the door behind them and glanced back to see if anyone noticed their departure. The guests seemed to be occupied with their conversations, and a few had departed to their chambers.

"Alex?" She looked at him curiously, then bit into her bottom lip.

Unable to control himself, he grabbed her arms and pulled her to him, then took her lips with his. She sighed into their kiss and leaned into him. She opened to him right away and when his tongue swept inside, his cock sprang to life. As much as it could beneath the confines of his skin-tight buckskin breeches. He pressed his body against hers, pulling her enticing front against his throbbing bulge.

Lily suddenly broke their kiss. "We can't do this."

He attempted to hide the pain of her rejection. "Of course, please forgive me. I overstepped. I expect nothing from you."

She glanced towards the door to the house and then turned her head back to face him. Lily took his hand in hers and electricity shot through each of his limbs. "It's just that anyone could see us. We aren't in private."

He observed the area, searching for a way he might kiss her again. He needed her kiss and the taste of her more than he had ever dreamt of needing another woman.

"Come with me," he whispered, pulling her hand to guide her to follow him. He noted the humor in the double meaning of his words and grinned to himself. He'd have to remember to write that down.

She willingly followed him as he led them both down the stairs of the terrace. They rounded the side of the house, and he pulled her across the lawn to a gazebo he had seen earlier that day when he followed her with Camden.

Once they were underneath the gazebo, he pulled her into his arms with all the need that built within him pining after her all day and pressed his lips to hers again. The intensity grew when she cupped her hand on his cheek and returned his kiss. His skin heated where she touched, reveling in the feel of her bare hand against his skin. If he reacted as such to her hand upon his cheek, he wasn't certain he would survive her touch in more sensitive places.

Every part of his body was aware of her, and the sweet sounds she made when she lost herself in their kisses. She pressed her body tighter against his, undulating herself against him.

He broke the kiss and rested his forehead against hers. "I want to touch you, love."

"Then touch me," she returned, her voice low and sultry.

"Did you like when I touched your breasts?"

She nodded against his forehead.

Needing no further invitation, he slipped his hand beneath her neckline and cupped her right breast. He feathered kisses along her neck as he palmed her round globe, feeling the bud of her nipple tighten beneath his hand.

When his lips were close to her ear, he whispered, "Have you ever touched yourself?"

"What do you mean?" she asked, rubbing her cheek against his.

"Between your legs, love," he said, sucking the lobe of her ear into his mouth, teasing it. "Have you ever slipped your hand there?"

She shook her head. "No. I know a man inserts himself there, but why would I touch myself in that place?"

He swallowed hard at her words, imagining what it would feel like to bury himself within her untouched heat.

"Do you trust me to give you your first taste of pleasure?" he asked, the hope evident in his tone. "You will remain a virgin in doing so." He wanted to be the one to introduce her to such things. To be the one who brought her to the brink of madness from her first climax. To be the one who wrote the pages of this chapter in her life.

"Yes, Alex," she said. "I feel like I need something. I ache there."

He pulled back so he could stare into her eyes. "Will you allow me to soothe that ache?"

"Please."

Alex kissed her again, walking her towards the backless bench that was behind her. He swooped her into his arms, not breaking their kiss, and then laid her longways across the bench. He positioned her legs so her feet rested on the ground on each side and her bottom almost hung off the end.

Gently lifting her skirts, Alex laid them to rest on her waist. Standing at the end of the bench, between her legs, he leaned his arm down and ran his fingers over her folds, and she gasped.

Watching her move and try to push herself against his hand, he thought she was the most beautiful, enticing woman he had ever seen. He circled the sensitive flesh above her folds with his fingers.

She arched her back. "Alex," she moaned.

"Alex, more? Or Alex, stop?" he asked, hoping more than anything that she would allow him to continue.

"Alex, more," she pleaded.

He trailed his fingers lower, exploring her core until he reached her wet cunt, slipping a finger inside of her. His cock warred against the buttons of his breeches at how tight she was. "You are so wet."

He moved his finger inside of her, and she rocked with his movements. Alex needed to taste her. He wanted to give her the most exquisite first orgasm that would radiate through her entire body. One that would make it difficult to walk from how her legs shook and tensed, from the way he licked, sucked, and loved her. Kneeling between her legs, he lowered his head to flick his tongue against her most sensitive place.

She released a loud moan, and her hands shot to his hair. He loved the feeling of her fingers gripping his head and he increased the intensity of the attention he gave with this mouth. He removed his finger and dipped his head lower so that his tongue slipped inside of her, and she moved against him in such a way that he knew she enjoyed and wanted everything he was doing.

Alex placed his free hand on her stomach to hold her in place against the bench, then used his other hand to slip two fingers inside of her, stretching her tight opening.

He worked his fingers inside of her while licking and sucking her sensitive flesh. Her moans and mumbles were unintelligible the closer she came to the peak of her climax. Alex glanced up at her and she writhed as much as she could beneath the hold he had on her.

"Are you ready for me to make you come?"

"I'm not certain I know what that means," she said, panting between each of her words.

"You are about to find out, love. Just let go and allow it to wash over you."

He returned his mouth to the opening of her slit and lathed it with his tongue, two fingers still moving within her. It only took a few more moments before she cried out and shattered from his touch, bucking beneath him. She moaned and cried out his name and some other words he didn't understand. He slowed his attention so she could ride the waves of pleasure for as long as possible until she stilled and relcased a sated sigh.

Alex withdrew his fingers and used both hands to spread her open further, exposing her wet cut to him, then ran his tongue from the bottom to the top, tasting the proof of her climax.

"Alex," she whispered.

As much as his cock hated him for it, he lowered her skirts and helped her to sit up on the bench so that he could sit beside her. "You taste so good." He placed several kisses along her neck.

She tilted her head to the side, giving him better access. "Isn't there something I can do for you? So you feel the same."

Alex's cock jumped at her words. "As much as I would enjoy doing more, we must return. We have been gone too long already." He could admit that he wanted her for himself and believed he would ask for her hand, but he didn't wish to risk them being caught together and removing her choice of a husband from her. His affection for her was far too great for that. She deserved to choose her future, and he wished to be chosen. More than anything, he wanted her to choose him.

Alex rose and pulled her to her feet to join him. He kissed her, hoping his kiss conveyed everything he felt. Hoping she somehow knew what his heart wished to speak to her.

"Can we speak tomorrow?" he asked after he broke the kiss.

"Of course." She placed another quick kiss on his lips.

He tucked a loose curl behind her ear. "Let's get you back inside."

With any luck, Lady Lily would soon agree to become his viscountess.

Chapter 8

The next day, Lily paced the terrace of the Ockhams' home. Lord Knox had asked to speak with her after they broke their fast, and she was almost certain he intended to offer for her.

Lily wasn't certain what to do. Her father had been clear in his direction to her. She must return from the house party betrothed to Lord Knox. That was what he expected of her. Legally, that was what her father would require her to do, whether or not she agreed.

The challenge was that she believed Alex had claimed pieces of her heart bit by bit, and it was only a matter of time before he had it all, if he hadn't already. His was the face that consumed her thoughts and dreams.

But she was certain that if Lord Knox offered for her, he was who her father was going to accept. Lord Knox was an earl, while Alex was a viscount. Although, hopefully, in the very distant future, Alex would be an earl one day as he was in succession to inherit his father's title.

The way Alex touched her the previous evening with his hands and mouth was even more delightful than Rosina had led her to believe. She wasn't certain that once with him would ever be enough. Worse, and as much as she wished to keep fighting the realization, she loved him. She was in love with Viscount Callan, and they could never be together.

Tears formed in the corners of her eyes as she continued to pace, thankful she found herself alone and away from the other guests. It seemed others at the house party would settle down in marriage with their perfect loves, but she would be subjected to a loveless marriage of convenience. Lord Knox's kind demeanor suggested that he would make a decent husband. But once she knew the depths of what love felt like, she wanted to be selfish and longed for a marriage filled with everything she knew she deserved.

Thanks to her encouragement, Lord Camden was upstairs, righting his wrongs with Lady Juliet, and another happy betrothal would be announced. While she was delighted for them to have found each other, her own heart was in a state of utter misery.

Lord Knox would seek her out at any moment, and she dreaded his appearance before her. She couldn't possibly say no, and that would be the end of any hope with the man she loved.

"Lily," a rich baritone said from behind her.

She discreetly wiped her eyes and drew a deep breath before she turned to face him.

"Alex," she whispered, unable to find any other words to say to him.

"What is the matter? Has something happened?"

She shook her head. "No. I must have something in my eye." Better to lie than to tell him what she feared. She didn't even know if he felt the same. Lust wasn't the same thing as love.

He eyed her curiously, and she wasn't certain if he believed her or not. She offered him a small smile, hoping he wouldn't ask her again or else she might crumble.

"I hoped we might discuss last night and our collective future," he said.

"You needn't feel obligated..." Shouting in the distance captured her attention, both of their heads turning in the direction of the sounds.

"Help! It's on fire," a voice could be heard shouting from the other side of the house, towards the stables.

Alex took off running down the stairs, and she followed behind him as quickly as she could. Once she reached the grass, they ran around the side of the house and saw one side of the stables on fire. Servants were bustling about, getting horses out to safety. Lord Demming ran into the burning stables, and Lily's heart raced faster from the perilous situation.

They were still a good distance away, but Alex didn't stop running, with Lily fast behind. Lord Knox appeared from the back entrance of the house, also running towards the entrance. He hollered after some of the men and then ran inside. Alex continued closer to the stables, which were ablaze, running straight towards the fire, and somehow she knew he would attempt to run into the building as well.

Lily increased her speed and worked to catch up with him. As he got closer to the deadly situation, she cried out after him. "No!"

He seemingly heard her and glanced over his shoulder. Seeing that she was following him and had almost caught up, he halted and turned around to grab her arms. Fear marred his handsome face.

"You must stay back."

She clutched the lapels of his jacket as if doing so would keep him from attempting to enter the building. "Come with me," she pleaded, her heart thumping so hard she believed he might see the movement in her chest.

He glanced at the opening. "I must try to assist."

"I won't let you." She gripped his lapels tighter.

Behind them, one corner of the building caved in, and smoke continued to overtake the area. She coughed as a few sparks caught the bottom of Lily's dress, a small flame starting on one of the ruffles. Alex panicked and began patting at her dress, ensuring that it was put out.

More sparks sprayed on them, and Lily began coughing from the proximity to the smoke. Alex swept her into his arms and carried her away from the scene.

She clasped her arms around his neck, and behind them she saw another corner collapse, one side of the building in flames. "They are still inside," she said to him. Once they were a safe distance away, he set her back on her feet, and they watched the entrance to the stables. She reached for his hand and held on to it, not caring if anyone should see her doing so.

Her heart raced, hoping that both men would emerge safely from the building. Seconds felt like hours as the grouping of guests watched. Finally, Lord Knox called for help at the entrance and a couple of grooms ran inside and immediately exited again, carrying Lord Demming with them. Lord Knox emerged behind them and then collapsed in the grass.

A group formed near where they took Lord Demming, with Alex moving closer. She stood at his side, and sadness washed over her at the sight of the man whose breathing was shallow.

Lord Knox ran the rest of the way to them, coughing when he reached the group. Alex attempted to keep him back, but Lord Knox pushed past him and dropped to Lord Demming's side. Lily cried, watching the scene unfold. The air was thick with fear as everyone dreaded the thought of losing the noble and heroic Lord Demming, who had been the first to rush into the building to save the others.

Finally, Demming coughed, and everyone breathed audible sighs of relief. There had been no people or horses lost in the fire, which was a miracle in itself. The stables would have to be rebuilt, but that was a far better outcome than loss of life.

Tears still streamed down her face, overwhelmed by the gravity of the situation and what might have occurred. Her shoulders shook, and she fought to regain her composure.

Alex noticed her emotion and clasped her hand again. "Come with me."

She nodded and let him lead her back inside. With the guests outside, they were alone in the house. It was so silent, one might have heard a pin drop. He turned her to face him, and her tears were unrelenting.

Cupping her cheek, he kissed her forehead. "Lily," he whispered before pulling back to look at her. His expression was pained at seeing her in such a state.

Alex picked her up, cradling her in his arms, and carried her from the room. She wrapped her arms around his neck and buried her face in his shoulder. He carried her to the stairs, then climbed them with her secure in his arms. When he reached the top of the staircase, he whispered in her ear, "Which chamber is yours?"

She picked up her head to point down the hallway to the door that would lead to her room.

He strode to the door, carrying her inside, and closed it behind him. She heard the turn of the lock before he carried her across the room to the settee. Alex sat down, still holding her across his lap.

Releasing all the emotion and fear of the moment, she sobbed into his neck.

"Shhh," he whispered, rubbing her back as if she were precious to him. "It's all right. All is well."

She was overcome by thinking about what might have happened, and as selfish as it was, what might have happened to Alex if he had run into the burning building. Even if she couldn't go against her father's wishes and marry Alex, she couldn't live if something had happened to him. It was a cruel twist of fate that she might have found love, and her father insisted she wed another man.

After several more sobs, Lily calmed herself but kept her head on his shoulder as they sat in silence for a few minutes.

"The events of the day would make a great scene in a play," he said, attempting to lighten the mood.

"Don't jest," she said, raising her head to meet his gaze. "I was frightened."

"I wouldn't have let any harm come to you." He ran his knuckles along her cheek.

She shook her head. "I was frightened for *you*. You were going to run in there, and…and…" she didn't finish and pressed her lips to his.

He parted his lips, and she slipped her tongue inside of his mouth until her tongue pressed against his. She tasted his tea from breakfast, reveling in the feel of his tongue as she recalled the wicked things he did with it the night before. The area between her thighs became damp, and she wrapped her arms tighter around his neck.

His hands moved and explored her body over her dress, settling his hand on her hip. He moved her against the bulge that pressed to her other hip. Breaking their kiss, he sucked the tender place on her neck.

"Alex," she whispered as he licked and sucked along the tops of her breasts. "I want you."

He ceased what he was doing and caught her gaze. "I don't think you know what you are saying, love."

She shifted her feet to the floor and removed herself from his lap. Turning to face him, she straddled him, placing a knee on the cushion on each side of his thighs. "My best friend is Rosina, and she told me quite a few things. I assure you, I know what I am saying." Before he could respond, she sat down on his lap and took his lips again. He clasped his arms around her, placing his palms flat against her back to hold her against him.

As she deepened their kiss, he began working the buttons on the back of her dress. Exploring every bit of his mouth with her tongue while he unfastened button after button until he slipped her gown down. She broke their kiss to pull her arms from the sleeves so her dress could be pushed down around her waist. She kissed his neck and jaw, loving the salty taste of his skin, while he worked to unlace her stays.

Once he loosened them enough, he lifted them from her body and tossed them aside, leaving her bare from the waist up before him.

Lowering his head, he took one of her tight buds into his mouth and sucked hard while both hands massaged and kneaded her breasts. She instinctively rocked on his lap, easing the ache between her legs by using his body to apply pressure to the place she never knew existed until he licked there.

He released a low growl and slipped one of his hands to her bottom to help her move against him. His breeches hardly hid the hard bulge between his legs that teased her through the fabric. He shifted his mouth to her other breast, sucking and flicking her nipple with his tongue.

"Alex," she whispered again, pleading.

He pulled his head up to look at her. "Are you certain?"

She nodded but then bit into her bottom lip, the doubt washing over her. "Unless you don't also want me."

He looked at her as if she had gone mad. "Sweetheart, I only want you to be sure. I assure you I would pick being with you over having air in my lungs." He reached between them and unbuttoned his falls, allowing his member to protrude between them.

Glancing down, she took in the sight of it, having never seen one in person before. It was much larger than she imagined, which made her mildly concerned knowing where it was expected to go. Lily placed her hand on it, longing to experience what it felt like. It was soft and smooth to the touch, but when she fisted her hand around it, it was like a steel rod.

Alex sucked in a breath of air when she felt along his shaft, and he licked his lips. "You feel how hard my cock is?" he whispered. "It is all for you."

She needed to see the rest of him and began undoing the buttons of his coat. He shrugged his arms out of his coat and then she helped him remove his waistcoat. She lowered her lips to his neck when she began unfastening each button of his shirt. After tossing his shirt aside, he was naked above the waist. Lily ran her hands along his taut chest. She ran her fingers through the light smattering of dark hair on his chest. "Your body is like that of a statue of Zeus."

He cupped her cheeks and placed a tender kiss on her lips. "That is a line from a Stormy Wells play."

She leaned down and kissed the top of his shoulder. "It doesn't make it any less true."

He rose to stand, taking her with him. She wrapped her arms around his neck, and he held her bottom as he carried her across the room to her bed.

Alex set her down gently and then laid her back across the coverlet. He pulled her dress down over her hips, then tossed it to the floor.

She shivered when the cool air reached her naked body, laid bare before him on the bed other than her stockings.

"You are perfect, love," he said, running his hand down her right leg, slowly removing her stocking. He placed a light kiss on the inside of her left thigh, his warm breath driving her wild, then removed the stocking from that leg.

He pushed his breeches down and kicked off his boots and socks, then scooted her further back on the bed. Alex climbed onto the bed with her, positioning himself on his knees between her legs. She watched him with interest and heavy-lidded desire when he lifted her legs and pressed her thighs so they were against her stomach, giving him full access to her most intimate, sensitive place. Holding her legs, he lowered his head and licked the wicked area that throbbed.

She moaned with each flick of his tongue. Then he shifted his head lower so that he pushed his tongue inside of her, while she was spread open before him. He flicked his tongue and she tried to rock against him as he held her steady.

"You are so deliciously wet," he said, raising his head. "Let's see if we can make you more so."

He returned his head between her legs and went even lower, running his tongue along the hole of her arse.

She gasped in shock. "Alex." But the wicked pleasure of his tongue there made her crave for more.

Unfortunately, he picked up his head. "Did you not enjoy that?"

"I did. Very much," she said. "I just didn't know...didn't know it felt good there."

He smirked at her. "Love, there are many things I can introduce you to, particularly there. But all in good time."

Lowering his head, he licked his way back to the wicked area again. That time he pushed the tip of his tongue inside, stretching her in a way that she never would have thought possible.

Using his left forearm, he held both her thighs and shifted his right hand between her legs, where he slid two fingers inside of her core. He continued the attention with his tongue on her arse and worked his fingers inside of her.

He removed his tongue and lifted his head, and she was disappointed to lose the sensation there. "You are so ready for me, if you still want me," he said, moving his fingers again. She moaned, and he lowered his head to suck and lick her nub. She had been so worked up, teetering on a precarious edge of bliss that a few more flicks of his tongue caused her to shatter and buck beneath him, cresting the peak of her climax. Moving herself against him, she fought to prolong the pleasure as long as she could.

He released her legs so that one was on each side of him. He hovered over her and leaned down to kiss her lips. Sweeping his tongue inside of her mouth, she tasted herself on his tongue when he pressed it against hers. His hard cock pressed against her, and she wanted to know how it would feel inside of her. "Please, Alex, I want you."

He feathered kisses along her jaw and neck, groaning from his own desire. When he reached her ear, he whispered, "I will do my best to keep from hurting you."

"I already know it hurts the first time, but I don't care."

He positioned himself at her opening, pressing the head of his shaft inside. The action was thrilling, and she pushed against him, wanting to take more.

"Wrap your legs around me, love."

She did as he said, and he pressed further in, kissing her in between each inch. He did so slowly, allowing her to adjust to him. The more he filled her up, the more her love for him radiated from her body. She wanted to join as one with him, to know what it felt like to be his, even if they would only have that one time together.

He pushed the rest of his length into her core, and there was a bit of pain. She closed her eyes, waiting for the pain to ease.

"Are you all right?" he asked, the worry evident from how his brow furrowed.

She blinked several times and locked onto his gaze, wondering at the tenderness in his expression. Could it be love? It appeared to be what she believed love might look like.

"Yes, I am all right." She pressed against him, ready for him to move.

He withdrew and then thrust himself completely inside of her again. The sensation was even better than she might have dreamt. Perhaps it was also how much she cared for the man who gave her such pleasure with his body.

The thought of never being with him again overtook her, and she wrapped her arms around him, wanting him closer to her. He shifted to hold himself up with his elbows, and she enjoyed the warmth of his torso pressed against hers, moving against her body with each thrust. He kissed her tenderly on her lips, then pulled back and stared into her eyes while he thrust into her with slow, tender movements.

She almost looked away, feeling slightly embarrassed being so exposed and vulnerable beneath him, but the intensity of the moment and her love for him kept her gaze locked on his, each thrust of his hips driving her closer to falling over the edge of something exquisite.

"Lily," he whispered. "This must be what heaven feels like."

With his slow, deep thrusts, he pushed her just to the peak of her orgasm and her eyes rolled back and she cried out when pleasure shot through her body in intense waves. "Alex," she moaned, convulsing beneath him.

He thrust into her a few more hard and quick times before he pulled out and warmth pooled on her stomach as he took her lips with his again, releasing small groans as he rocked against her.

After he took a few heavy breaths and kissed her forehead, Alex rose from the bed. She watched as he retrieved a cloth from the washbasin and was instantly cold from the loss of his body against hers. Even worse, the realization that she would never be with him in such a way again.

Lily willed herself not to cry. She could do so once he departed. And she would, probably all night long.

He returned and gently wiped between her legs. "There was blood from your first time. I can take the cloth with me so your maid won't see it and become suspicious." He wiped her stomach and then used the cloth on himself. Lily sat up in the bed and watched the way the muscles of his back and arms flexed as he moved, and it made her want him again. Her skin heated, and she fought the urge to pull him back into the bed with her.

The tears threatened to fall again, knowing it wasn't meant to be. Once Lord Knox proposed, she wouldn't allow another man in her bed, no matter how much she wished for Alex to never leave her side. Her father wouldn't allow her to refuse Lord Knox's proposal, and she couldn't go against her father. No one did. And even if she could, legally it wouldn't matter.

Her situation rivaled the most tragic of Shakespearean plays. A realization she might have found ironic if it were happening to anyone else, but she better understood heartbreak in a way she hadn't appreciated before.

Alex slipped his breeches up over his hips and buttoned them. He glanced at her, then opened his mouth as if he wished to say something and then closed it again. Drawing a deep breath, he knelt to the floor beside the bed and clasped her hand.

Oh no, he couldn't intend to ask for her. The ironic tragedy of the situation drove the knife deeper into her heart.

Chapter 9

Alex was on his knee, naked from the waist up before the woman he loved. He hadn't doubted for a moment he was in love with her before they had lain together. Being with her in that way only confirmed the depths of his feelings and that he must have her in his life forever.

"Lily, I know it may seem fast and mad, but I am falling in love with you. And, given what has occurred between us, I am inclined to believe that you might care for me, too," he said, rubbing his thumb along her hand that he held in his. "Will you marry me?"

He stared at her, expecting her to throw her arms around his neck and delight in the heartfelt profession of his love and that he wished to marry her. Several seconds passed, and his entire body tensed, and he did his best not to let his expression convey the same. His heart was in his throat, watching her appear to be at war with her thoughts. Had he misread everything between them? No, he couldn't. He was just inside of her only minutes ago.

Alex stared into her eyes, and his smile faltered further with each additional second that it took her to muster her response.

"No, Alex. I will not marry you."

He rose to his feet and paced along the side of the bed. Unsure if he heard her correctly and trying to make sense of what had occurred between them.

"But I love you," he finally said.

She said nothing and clasped her hands in front of her naked body. She wrung and squeezed her fingers, and it only put him in an even greater state of unease.

"Are you telling me you feel nothing for me?" he asked, almost pleading, begging her to feel the same that he did, or even enough to give them a chance.

"Alex," she whispered.

He held his hand up to silence her. "Tell me. Tell me that there is no part of your heart that is mine." Surely she wasn't without any feelings for him. Their meeting had to have been the work of fate, a story he would have told across a hundred pages. This couldn't be how their story ended. They were a romantic comedy, not a tragedy.

Lily's expression was one of sadness and there were tears that formed at the corners of her eyes. He longed to press his lips to her salty tears and tell her he loved her again, but he had already played the part of the lovesick fool once before. Although he would do so again if she didn't give him a good reason why they couldn't be together.

She swallowed hard and found her voice. "I will marry Lord Knox."

He fought all the rage that boiled within him that he had found himself in another situation where he wasn't good enough to be the one chosen. Believing he had found the woman he would wed, and then she married someone else. At least he hadn't bedded that one. His hands formed tight fists. "You encouraged me into your bed when you were engaged to another?"

"No," she blurted. "He hasn't asked yet."

He released his fists and allowed his shoulders to lower. If she wasn't engaged, he had a chance. "Then marry me, Lily. There is nothing standing between us."

"He intends to ask, and I will say yes."

"Why?" Nothing made sense. His world was spinning, and his stomach tightened and knotted every second that Lily didn't say that she felt something for him, and not Knox.

"It doesn't matter why, Alex. The end result is the same." She raised her chin and drew a deep breath.

"Tell me. I want to hear the reason." He couldn't let her off that easily. There was something else going on. He knew it in his heart.

She looked at him, and a tear rolled down her right cheek. She opened her mouth to speak and closed it again, then she began speaking in another language.

Alex thought it might have been German, but he wasn't proficient in the language.

"Lily, tell me what you just said," he pleaded. "In English this time."

She shook her head, and he knew she was fighting back more tears.

Alex grabbed his shirt and slid it onto his body before buttoning it. He donned his boots and picked up his coats. His movements were abrupt, doing his best to hold back the anger brewing within him again. He stuffed the cloth he used to clean them both in his pocket.

"I can't believe I did this again. I am questioning if I even know you," he said, rising and moving towards the door. "I'll never understand how you could be so cruel to invite me to your bed and then tell me you intend to marry another man."

He didn't give her a chance to respond and he couldn't look back at her. Unlocking the door, he poked his head out to check the hallway, then departed, needing to put as much distance between them as possible. Given the state of his dress and how in disarray he was, he quickly made his way to his chamber.

The only good thing from the last few minutes was that he believed he went unseen by one of the other guests.

Alex leaned against the door of his chamber after he locked it behind himself. She'd turned him down. Lily gave him her virginity and the most intense, ardent experience he'd ever shared with a woman, then she refused to marry him.

His heart had been ripped in half and every muscle in his body ached from the pain of her rejection. After what they had experienced together, there hadn't been a doubt in his mind that she would have agreed to marry him. Then they could have planned to announce their betrothal later that evening, but she'd crushed his entire heart and soul when she'd said no.

None of it made any sense. She had to feel something for him. His Lily wasn't cold and unfeeling. He recalled the way she looked at him when she refused to allow him to enter the burning stables. She hadn't stopped or called after Knox. She called after him. Alex.

When she spoke what he believed to be German, there was something in her expression and the emotion in her words that he was inclined to believe that she did, in fact, love him. Perhaps it was wishful thinking on his part, but if she didn't love him, wouldn't she just say so?

If she held any feelings for Lord Knox, wouldn't she have also said that? Wouldn't she have taken Knox to her bed instead of him?

The mental image of her taking another man to bed caused bile to rise in his throat. He couldn't allow her to marry someone else. He couldn't allow another man to touch her in all the ways he had. She was his, and he'd determine what held her back and then help her see that whatever it was did not signify for their future. There was nothing that would be strong enough to keep him from her, and the sooner she accepted that, the better.

Moving across the room, Alex dropped into the chair at the writing desk in his chamber. He ran his hands down his face and rested his elbows on the desk before him, propping his chin in his hands. He drew a deep breath and picked up his quill. If he were to write the event into his play, he'd certainly give them a far happier ending.

Alex tapped his quill against his cheek, replaying the conversation with Lily in his head again. It didn't add up. He thought about it for every bit of a half an hour. Analyzing every word she said, at least the ones in a language he could understand.

The only thing he could come up with was that he must speak to Knox. Perhaps if he could ascertain the gentleman's intentions, he could convince Knox to aban-don his plans to wed Lily if it came to that. And if the man didn't readily agree, well, Alex would cross that bridge when he came to it, but he would not give up on her.

He would do whatever it took to give them both a chance at a life together.

Chapter 10

The next morning, Alex hoped he might speak with Knox right away. Better to tackle the matter head-on before the man spoke with Lily and did something disastrous like propose to her. He couldn't allow that to happen. If he believed she loved or cared for the man, he loved her enough to step aside, but there was something in her reaction that told him it wasn't the case. It seemed more likely to him that she believed, for some reason—probably related to her father—that she must marry Knox.

Alex learnt from his valet the previous evening that Knox would take a tray in his room, so Alex did the same. He didn't wish to encounter Lily so soon after she rejected him. The small silver lining to his broken heart was that he used the angst and turmoil in the play he was writing. He had crafted a character inspired by Lily, and if he couldn't get her to see that they belonged together, he could rectify their situation on the page. Doing so gave him a bit of satisfaction and even a bit of hope.

Joining the rest of the guests for breakfast, he glanced down at the table, looking for Knox. The dratted man wasn't there, but Lily was. He wasn't certain if she saw him or not, as he glanced away from her and went to the sideboard. Once he made his selections, he sat at the far end of the table on the same side as her. The seating eliminated the chance of staring at her during the meal, which would be for the best. Even though she looked even more beautiful than he recalled in his dreams, in the two-second glance he allowed himself to have of her that morning.

His heart ached, and if he were less in control of his actions, he would pull her from the table and throw her over his shoulder in front of everyone, marking her as his in their eyes. While he did give that idea more consideration than he ought, he needed her to choose him. He knew he deserved to be chosen the same as his heart had chosen her.

He ate quietly, avoiding the polite small talk from the guests sitting around him. As soon as he had cleared his plate, he departed the breakfast room without so much as a glance back.

Alex rang for his valet and asked him to alert Knox's valet that Alex wished to speak with him as soon as possible, requesting Knox to meet him in the library. No more waiting, and no more trying to happen upon him. And if Knox didn't come down soon, Alex was going to break down the man's chamber door.

After an hour of pacing the library, Knox finally appeared. "You wished to speak with me?"

Alex whirled around to face him. He noted the man wore a joyous smile, almost as if he had been engaged in more-than-satisfying bed sport. Perhaps he had, which would explain why he hid away in his chamber, or in someone else's. It was a common occurrence at house parties.

Alex couldn't judge the man, given he had done the same thing, and with an innocent. And he'd be lying to himself if he didn't acknowledge that he walked around half-erect from wanting her again. But if Knox was entertaining someone else and then intended to ask for Lily's hand, that would earn the man a facer. Or ten.

"I wish to know what your intentions are towards Lady Lily." He might as well get straight to the heart of the matter. Alex had no patience for pleasantries and pretense, not when his future with Lily hung in the balance.

Knox gave him an amused expression. "Do you mean to tell me that you are in love with her, Callan?"

"Yes," he replied, taking a few steps closer. "I wish to marry her, but she seems to believe you intend to propose."

He seemed to contemplate what Alex said. "She can't have affection for me, as she's given no indication of such. Perhaps she doesn't return your affections, Callan."

Alex clenched his fists at the man's words. "I have reason to believe she does," he ground out.

The man laughed, not cruelly, but in one that indicated he found Alex amusing, and it took everything Alex had not to proceed with his plan to plant him that facer he had considered, until Knox finally spoke. "I do not intend to propose, my good man. I intended to speak with her today to inform her of such. Then it shall be up to you to win her."

Alex released a long, relieved breath that he wouldn't have to do something more severe to prevent Knox from attempting to take Lily away from him. "Why did you allow her to believe you were interested if you weren't?" He shouldn't care since the man wouldn't be an issue, but something about the matter didn't sit right with him.

"Her father," Knox said, the smile leaving his face. "The man was quite insistent, and he was difficult to refuse."

Alex nodded in understanding. Just another reason for Alex to dislike Lily's parents.

Knox took the last couple of steps to where Alex stood and grabbed his shoulder. "For what it's worth, I hope you succeed at winning her hand."

Alex's heart clenched at the mere thought of what it would mean if he failed. "I must."

"I will speak with her as soon as I can."

Relief washed over Alex that Knox wouldn't offer for Lily. He still had to be sure that she wanted to be with him, but Knox would remove an enormous obstacle from their path.

"Thank you," Alex replied. Both men started towards the exit. "If our hosts are looking for me, I shall be in my chamber. I have some matters to tend to." Those matters included avoiding Lily, at least for the time being, and picking up work where he left off writing his play while he thought of what he'd say to her.

Alex took off towards the stairs, needing to get his thoughts on paper and prepare to speak with Lily again. Even though she had broken his heart when she rejected him, once he found the right words to ask her again, he hoped with everything in his soul that she wouldn't refuse him.

Chapter 11

Lily wasn't sure how she had appeared presentable to face the day and attend breakfast with the rest of the house party. Every part of her body had been aware when he entered the room, but she couldn't bring herself to look at him. If she caught his gaze, he would see it on her face and in her eyes. He would see the love she had for him, and he wouldn't accept that they didn't have a future together.

After she had refused Alex the day prior, she cried for so long that Posy had been worried about her and insisted she take a tray in her room for dinner. She didn't even bother to poke at the food for Posy's sake, leaving it untouched.

She had been a fool for thinking that experiencing such love and pleasure in his arms would allow her to carry on in a marriage she didn't want. It might have been more palatable if Alex hadn't told her he loved her. She might have been able to convince herself that he was another man who wanted to use her body and move on to his next conquest. But he'd told her everything she had dreamt of hearing and what she had longed to say to him in return.

Lily hated that she had allowed him to believe she didn't feel the same. The hurt that marred his expression had broken her heart into so many pieces, it might never be mended again.

"What is the matter?" Rosina asked.

The pair had gone for a long walk since they had spent little time in each other's company during the house party thus far. Rosina had been taken with her own pursuits, and Lily was a bit envious of her friend's far simpler existence.

"It's nothing."

Rosina grabbed her arm and pulled her to a stop. "What is going on, Lily?" she asked, then assessed her friend with concern. "You are trembling. Did someone do something untoward?" The anger in Rosina's voice was touching, given that she knew her friend would give anyone in attendance a firm set down on her behalf.

"I must marry Lord Knox," Lily sobbed, unable to hold back the emotion.

"If he did something to you…"

Lily shook her head. "No, it's nothing like that. I love Lord Callan. Alex."

Realization washed over Rosina's face. "Dearest, have you been"—she paused to scan the area to confirm that no one was in earshot—"intimate with Callan?"

Lily drew a deep breath and nodded.

Rosina clasped her hand and squeezed it. "You do not have to marry Knox if that is not what you wish to do."

"But my father—"

"To hell with your father," Rosina said, cutting her off. "Go to Gretna Green if your father doesn't agree. It matters not what your father and Knox had discussed. Assuming Callan wishes to marry you." Her face hardened again. "Because if he dallied with you and toyed with your affections, he has another thing coming."

Lily released a puff of air. "He asked me to marry him, and he says he loves me."

"And you refused him?"

"Yes. Right after we…"

Rosina drew a deep breath. "His pride may be a bit wounded, which is typical of a man who faces rejection. But if he loves you, he will do what is necessary to have you, even if that means convincing your father to allow him to do so or the scandal of eloping to Scotland. But do not marry a man you don't love." Her words were laced with emotion.

Lily squeezed her friend's hand. "You still miss him. Your husband."

Rosina gave her a somber nod. "And that is why I know you deserve love, and if Callan loves you, you must fight. Fight whatever stands in your path because love doesn't come around often."

She noted Rosina appeared to be struggling with something, and she wasn't certain it had to do with her husband.

"Do you have feelings for the duke, Rosina?"

Rosina flinched as if Lily had struck her. "What? We're talking about you," Rosina said, waving her off. "What are you going to do to make things right with Callan?"

"I suppose I must speak with Knox and then confirm if Alex still wishes to marry me."

Suddenly, she recalled something he said about doing the same thing again. That realization brought their conversation about broken hearts crashing back into her like a ton of bricks. He'd had his heart broken before, and then Lily had refused him. She had made a mess of everything and needed to set things to their rights. Rosina was right. To hell with her father.

"I must go. I will see you later," Lily called out to her friend as she hurried away. She didn't wait for a response and made her way back to the terrace and reentered the salon. Thinking about what she would say to Alex.

A life with him was the only future she wanted and thus the only one she would entertain. If he loved her as he said he did, he would move mountains to be with her, and that just might be what was needed.

"My lady," a familiar voice called to her when she returned to the salon.

"Lord Knox," she said, giving him a polite nod. She was relieved to see him so she could inform him that she would not marry him.

"We never got to speak yesterday after all the unfortunate events. Might I be able to speak with you now?"

She inhaled a fortifying breath and nodded. "I would like to speak with you as well."

He took her hand and placed it in the crook of his arm, then led her back to the terrace. "I think it best if we have a bit of privacy."

She steadied herself. He was going to propose, and she'd have to decline another man in less than a day. He might get angry at her and write to her father. She and Alex may have to leave the house party immediately if she could convince him to do so. Lily shook off her thoughts and tried to force herself to listen to what Knox had to say.

Once they were on the far corner of the terrace, he gave a tender smile and finally spoke. "Are you in love with Lord Callan?"

Had she heard him correctly? Why would he ask her that? There was warmth in his voice, a genuine sympathy that replaced any hint of anger or hurt she might have expected from him.

"Yes," she said, her voice barely above a whisper.

He nodded as if she had confirmed what he already knew. "And you wish to marry him?"

"More than anything," she said, allowing her heart to hope that it would be the case for them.

Lord Knox grinned at her. "Then marry him."

"But—"

"I don't intend to offer marriage after all, my lady. You are intelligent, charming, and beautiful, and you will make a wonderful wife for Callan, not me."

She swallowed hard, unsure she believed what she heard. "But you arranged things with my father."

"We signed no contracts. I will write to him right away, and I will encourage him to support the match with Callan."

Unable to stop herself, she threw her arms around Lord Knox's neck. "Thank you. Thank you so much." The action was far too forward and not typically done, but he didn't push her away. He gave her back a soft pat and then she released him. "How did you know about my affection for Lord Callan?"

"Your gentleman spoke with me. He seems quite determined. I believe you have yourself a good man, there."

"You are also a good man, Lord Knox. I hope you find someone as well," she said, her eyes turning glassy.

"Call me George, please," he said. "And don't you worry about me. Just make things right with Callan. Perhaps I'll even get an invitation to the wedding." He flashed her a grin riddled with mirth.

"Of course, George. Well, if he will have me. I already rejected his proposal."

His expression turned to a knowing stare. "I don't think you have to worry about that."

"If you will excuse me," Lily said. "I must find him right away."

He extended his arm to her. "I'll do better than that. I know where he is, and I'll take you to him."

She took his arm and allowed him to lead her through the house. They ascended the grand staircase, and she suspected Alex must be in his chamber. They navigated to one of the other wings of rooms opposite from where her chamber was. Once they reached a large white door, George nodded towards it.

"Good luck, Lily," he said, grinning at her.

"Thank you, George." Lily squeezed George's hand and then released his arm as he backed away.

She closed her eyes and drew a long breath before trying the handle and quietly entering Alex's chamber. She closed the door behind her without making a sound. Scanning the room, she found him hunched over his writing desk, lost in thought as his quill glided across the parchment.

Lily took a few steps closer to him and stopped again to watch him work. Some of his hair had fallen across his forehead and he rubbed the back of his neck as if he were working out a bit of tension but didn't stop writing. She could have watched him do so all day and been more than content.

Unable to help herself, she noted he had dispensed with his coats and cravat, and her knowledge of what he looked like beneath his shirt caused her entire body to heat. She sighed, and his head jerked towards her.

"Lily," he exclaimed, jumping to his feet. "What are you doing here?"

Lily clasped her hands in front of her and raised her chin. "I came to ask you to marry me."

"What?"

She stepped closer to him so there was only about a foot of space between their bodies. "I wish to marry you."

He stared at her with a range of emotions reflected in his eyes. Hurt, disbelief, pride, love. "Lily…"

"I love you, Alex. I had resigned myself to being a spinster and believed the closest I would get to love was watching it on the theatre stage. My father commanded me to leave this house party betrothed to Lord Knox. But I will only marry you. I'm sorry that I didn't jump into your arms and speak the words when you asked. I only hope you can forgive me because I shall love you every day for the rest of my life."

Chapter 12

Alex reached for Lily and pulled her against him. He was half afraid that he was dreaming and that his angel was teasing him in his sleep, so he needed to feel her in his arms to confirm that she was real. "I was prepared to spend every minute of every day working to convince you of the very thing." He lowered his head and pressed his lips to hers, pleased that she immediately opened to him so he could taste her tongue against his.

She took control of the kiss, wrapping her arms around his neck and pulling herself closer against his body, which was already on fire for her. She undulated against him, and he almost questioned how she had so quickly become a tempting little vixen. He'd delight in knowing he was the recipient of all of her wanton desires.

She pulled her lips away from his. "You didn't answer me."

"Yes, love. I'm marrying you. And if your father wishes to question if you are mine, I shall do what I must to bring him around to my way of thinking."

Lily pressed against him and walked him backwards to the chair in front of his desk and urged him to sit. "Let us not speak of my father just now."

She placed a hand on each of his thighs to support herself and leaned forward to place a few kisses along his lips. "Remove your shirt."

He didn't even question it, making quick work of the buttons and tossing the shirt to the side.

She ran her hands along his chest, and his muscles flexed beneath her touch. Her hands were so soft, and the intoxicating scent of vanilla from her proximity caused his head to fall back. She took advantage and licked and sucked at his neck. His cock fought hard against his breeches, and he rocked his hips, moving himself against the fabric.

Her lips and touch disappeared, and when he lifted his head, she had knelt before him and begun massaging his thighs.

"What are you doing?" The words came out with a sigh. Hoping she would take him into her sweet, beautiful mouth, he licked his lips, watching her reach for the buttons of his falls.

"I'm going to taste my future husband."

Her hands brushed against him through his breeches as she worked the buttons, and he almost came undone. He'd let her have her fun, and then he fully intended to find himself inside of her again.

His cock jutted into her hand when she released him, and he sucked in a breath from her soft hands moving along his shaft. She lowered her head and licked the liquid that had already escaped the tip. Watching her tongue lick around the tip of his cock was almost more than he could handle.

"Do I do it like this?" she asked before she took in half of his length and closed her mouth around it, sucking him into her mouth.

He clasped her head. "Yes. Just like that." Alex held her head in place and rocked in the chair so that his cock moved in and out of her mouth. She glanced up at him through her gold-rimmed spectacles, and the heat in her gaze almost set him on fire. He kept his eyes fixed on her, taking him that way, knowing he would spend in her mouth if she continued. As appealing as the thought was, he needed to be inside of her, to feel her body against his, and to know that they would always be together. That she was his, and he was hers.

He pulled her head further off him. "Come here, love."

She rose, and he lifted her skirts so she could straddle him. When she sat on his lap, facing him, his shaft rubbed against her. He slid his hand between them and guided two fingers inside of her. She was dripping and ready for him, and he groaned at the realization.

"I think you enjoyed sucking my cock."

She nodded and leaned against him, exploring his body with her hands and kissing her way to his ear. "Very much so."

Unable to wait any longer, he lifted her up and speared her with his entire length, eliciting a loud moan from her lips. He held her hips and rocked her on top of him, thrusting himself so each movement fully sheathed him inside of her wet heat.

He didn't have the control of his movements he wanted from their position in the chair. So he clasped her bottom against him and stood, not removing himself from her.

"Tighten your legs around me, love."

He held on to her bottom and began thrusting into her where he stood. Shifting her to bounce on top of him with each of his thrusts, penetrating her so deep he almost saw stars. She held on to him around his neck and took his lips, kissing him with such fervor, his body responded by bouncing her harder and faster.

"I need to lay you down," he ground out against her lips. "I am going to spend inside you if I continue."

"Don't stop," she pleaded. "I want this. I'm marrying you."

Her words made him come unhinged, and he gave her everything he had. She gripped his neck tighter, and her core tightened and pulsated around him when her orgasm came. "Alex," she moaned into his neck, her teeth grazing his shoulder.

He thrust into her twice more and then held her hips in place tight against him when he released his seed deep inside of her. He'd never released himself inside of a woman before, given he had never wanted to risk the chance of a babe, and the intensity from doing so made his legs wobbly.

She went limp in his arms. Her head rested on his shoulder, and he continued to stand there, holding her against him, wrapping his arms around her as if she were the most precious thing in the world. Because she was. He kissed her neck, then her cheek and jaw. "I love you, Lily."

Lily gripped him tighter. "I love you, too, Alex."

He carried her to the bed and sat her down, withdrawing himself from her. He tucked himself back into his breeches and rebuttoned them.

"Your dress is quite wrinkled," he said, grinning at her. "I believe you will have to sneak to your room to change before you rejoin the others."

"I don't want to leave you."

He leaned down and kissed her brow. "Then don't. I don't care about your wrinkled dress. It's a reminder that I've done my job to ensure you are a well-loved and well-bedded woman."

"I don't recall being in bed until now," she said, smirking at him.

"Am I to believe that you are disappointed then, my lady?"

She climbed off the bed to stand before him, wrapping her arms around his waist. "Not at all. Knowing how strong you are only makes me more wanton."

"Well, I am happy to tend to your needs in any way you see fit."

She laughed and playfully swatted at him, moving to sit in the chair at his desk. "I will need you to introduce me to all my options for doing so."

He had barely recovered from what they had just done, but he wanted her again. "We need to discuss our plans to marry. You may soon carry our babe, and that risk will only grow greater the longer we delay making you my wife. Because even now I'm thinking about in what position I want to come inside of you next."

Lily blushed at his words, and the flushed skin beneath her adorable freckles did nothing to ease his desire.

"You should write to my father right away. He won't give a fig what I want, but if you express your desire to marry quickly and join our families. He will respond to your title and that of your father's. And with Knox no longer an option, perhaps Papa will agree." She wrinkled her nose and glanced away. "He wanted the highest title, but his disappointing, plain, bluestocking daughter was a failure during her season."

He rushed to her side and clasped her hands. "There is nothing disappointing or plain about you. It is to my good fortune that no one else took notice of what was before them, and not because you are lacking. Your parents lack any sound sense and judgement, and they will not be allowed in your presence if they cannot show you the respect you deserve."

"You really must love me," she said, almost as if she had finally accepted it. Her expression changed as she contemplated him. "You said something yesterday. Something about how you did the same thing again. Were you in love before?"

Alex had slipped when he said that out of frustration, but leave it to his Lily to notice. "I believed myself to be in love before, yes. But I asked for her hand, and she declined because she had captured the attention of a duke."

Lily winced and wrung her hands together. He could see the guilt marring her expression from her rejection of his original proposal.

He knelt before her. "The situations aren't the same, my love. I only believed myself to be in love then and now I know that could never have been the case now that I have met you. And I know you didn't truly wish to marry Knox. That was the work of your father."

Alex took her hands in his and looked up at her. "I didn't know it was possible to love another person so much. I would meet your father at the dueling grounds if that is what you wished for me to do to right the wrongs he had done to you." He grinned at her and chuckled to himself. "I would give my life for yours if it would ease even the slightest pain you have endured."

She shook her head and laughed. "Now look who's quoting Stormy Wells." She glanced at the papers on his desk.

"About that, love. There is something else we should discuss."

She picked up the parchment and then read the one beneath it. "What is this?" She kept skimming the pages and then picked up another one.

"Lily…"

She had a character sheet in her hand that would be unmistakable where the inspiration came from.

"Are you writing about me? Or at least a character like me. The red hair and spectacles seem to be a bit too much of a coincidence."

"I was inspired by you. In awe of you. I still am, and I always will be."

She stared at him in disbelief. He wasn't sure if the expression was one of anger or not.

"When we met, did you only get close to me so you could write about me?"

He clasped her hips, still kneeling before her. "No, sweetheart. I promise. I turned you into a character to work through my feelings for you. Writing is how I think and process things."

"What were you going to do with these?"

"A man in love is just a man. It doesn't matter if he is a duke or a pauper, if the woman he loves doesn't return his affection, his life is diminished to nothing of worth."

"Why are you quoting lines from *Duke About Town* to me?"

He drew a deep breath, steadying himself for what he must reveal. For what he'd never revealed to anyone before. "I'm Stormy Wells."

She gasped and brought her hand to her mouth. "You don't jest?"

He shook his head. "No, love. You are the only person in the entire world besides my solicitor who knows."

Alex sat quietly and watched her process the impact of learning his identity.

"I just can't believe it," she finally said.

"It started as something I did to make sense of our world, and then I found I enjoyed creating stories and how people would interact in different scenarios in our society. I wrote my first play and had my solicitor send it to a playhouse, not expecting anything to happen. They wanted to buy it. The show was so popular, they came back to my solicitor asking to meet me. When I refused, they asked for more of my work. I never expected the plays to become as popular as they did. My solicitor protects my identity and I just write the stories I am compelled to tell."

She stared at him with awe and admiration. He sagged against her a bit in relief that it didn't appear she would change her mind about marrying him after learning his biggest secret.

"You must have made a small fortune."

He shrugged. "I donated all of it. My solicitor sees the funds are given to the orphanages and charities in the most need. I am already wealthy enough, and all I care about now is that you will still have me."

"Alex, it only makes me love you more for how brilliant you are."

He brought her hand to his lips. "You are the brilliant one. Perhaps with you at my side, we can translate the plays into other languages and earn even more funds for the charities."

"You would let me work with you?" she asked, shock and delight evident on her beautiful visage.

"I wish to share every aspect of our lives together, love."

Her eyes grew wide. "Does this mean I get to read your plays before they go to the solicitor?"

"Of course. Anything you wish, you shall have."

She leaned forward and placed a tender kiss on his lips. "You shall be the very best husband."

He rose and picked her up off the chair, took the seat for himself, and settled her across his lap. "Let's work on this letter to your father, and then I'll show you more of the husband I intend to be."

Epilogue

6 MONTHS LATER

Lily rubbed her rounded belly. Her stomach protruded enough that it was undeniable that she carried a sweet little one. Given how often she enjoyed her husband, it was no surprise that they had conceived almost right away.

The sun was high outside the drawing room window of their country estate, and she watched a few birds outside the window, distracting herself from reading the new book Alex had ordered for her. She still couldn't believe she had been so lucky to marry him.

Her father didn't resist the match, especially given that George had withdrawn his interest. But Alex gave her father a firm set down the first time he said something unkind about her. Alex's parents adored Lily, especially given that in their eyes she got their son to settle down and start making an heir. Alex's father even threatened to give her father the cut direct if he should say anything disparaging about Lily. Since then, her father and mother had both been on their best behavior and she could forgive them for treating her the way they had.

Alex strode into the room, saying nothing to her, and came straight to where she sat and scooped her up. He cradled her in his arms and carried her away.

"What on earth are you doing?"

"I have a surprise for you."

"I can walk, you know."

He shook his head. "You need all the rest you can get in your condition."

She laughed at him and clasped her hands around his neck. "You are impossible."

Alex would be the most devoted father. He would encourage his children and help them pursue whatever they wished. Very unlike what she had experienced growing up.

He carried her to his study and kicked his door closed behind them when they crossed the threshold. He sat her on top of his desk. "Close your eyes."

She did as he said, waiting for what he would do next.

"All right, open them."

Lily blinked her eyes open, and he held out a stack of parchment, tied together with twine and then a pink ribbon tied around it in a bow.

She eyed the stack in his hands and then glanced at him, catching his gaze.

"It's my next play. I am giving it to you to read first." He beamed at her, and she radiated with pride for her talented husband.

She took the bundle from his hands and glanced at the title, *The Viscount and the Wallflower.*

"This is about us?" she asked.

"Well, I changed enough details so that only we would know and added a bit of flourish. And I might have omitted a few titillating moments," he said, winking at her.

She wrapped one arm around his neck. "I love you so much." She released him and held the stack of parchment with both hands. "I can't wait to read it."

He snatched the bundle from her and set it on the bookcase behind him, next to the framed drawing that Lord Camden had done of her. She still found it humorous that Alex had followed them outside and then got Camden to give him the drawing.

"I'm afraid that has to wait," Alex said, kissing her neck. "I thought we might celebrate the conclusion of the play with a bit of a finish of our own."

Alex pressed himself between her legs, raising her skirts so that she was exposed to him.

"I thought I needed rest," she teased, giggling at him.

He urged her to lie back on the desk, grinning at her. "I shall do all the work."

Before she could object, not that she would, he dipped his head and had his tongue massaging the sensitive place above her core. She arched her back off the desk and moaned. No matter how many times he tasted her, each time was just as good as the last.

He spread her legs wider and ran his tongue down until it was inside of her. Her hands flung to his head, and she held him in place, rocking her cunt against his face. He pulled back and inserted two fingers where his tongue had been.

"I have the most perfect wife."

She moaned at how he moved his fingers inside her. "I want you, husband."

"I noticed," he said, grinning at her. He withdrew his fingers and brought them to her lips. She wasn't sure when he had freed himself from his breeches, but as she sucked his fingers into her mouth, he thrust himself inside of her. The sensation of it made her suck his fingers harder, and he released a low growl.

He brought his hand back and shifted her legs so her thighs were spread wide, and he supported them with his arms as he thrust into her. She moaned and whispered his name.

"Massage your breasts."

She did as he instructed, lifting her breasts from her stays so that they were visible over the neckline of her dress. She cupped them both, kneading as he moved inside of her. When she ran her thumbs along the tight buds of her nipples, she moaned.

"Just like that," he said, increasing his speed and pulling her thighs even tighter against him.

After a few more thrusts, she shattered beneath him. She didn't muffle her loud moans as she shook and savored her perfect fall over to the other side of her orgasm.

He didn't relent and buried himself deep inside of her. Releasing her thighs, he shifted his hands up to her breasts, massaging them for himself as he spent inside of her, slowing to a gentle rock of his hips.

Alex leaned over her and kissed her with her back pressed into the desk and his cock still inside of her.

"I should finish a play more often."

He withdrew and then helped her to sit back up on the desk, lowering her skirts back over her legs.

"Well, given how many times you've had me on top of this very desk," she said, tucking her breasts back into her stays, "I would say you don't need such an excuse."

He kissed her nose. "You've caught me."

Alex buttoned his falls, then grabbed the papers from behind him and handed them back to her. He scooped her up and carried her to the settee. She wouldn't even pretend she didn't adore the attention he lavished upon her because she did. Lily loved everything about the way Alex loved her.

He seated them both so they sat longways, with her positioned between his legs and leaning against him, her back against his front. The fire roared before them and it was the perfect, cozy moment. He kissed the top of her head as she untied the bow around the papers.

Beneath the title, there was a dedication.

To a certain woman: You are as precious as a flower, but you were never a wallflower. You have always shone from the center of the stage from the moment I first laid my eyes on you, and you are forever in possession of my heart.

The tears rolled down her cheeks, and she glanced up at him to see him grinning at her.

He shifted one hand to cup her rounded stomach, using his thumb to massage where their precious babe grew.

"Keep reading, sweetheart."

Want more of Alex and Lily?

They have appearances in the other books in the Unlikely Betrothal series! If you haven't met Nick and Eliza from *The Earl and the Vixen*, then get your copy today!

Here is a look at the full series, and keep reading for a sneak peek at *The Duke and the Widow*, which will feature James and Rosina!

The Unlikely Betrothal Series

A different couple at the same house party finds their match! Who will be next? Each of these books are stand-alone stories complete with a HEA and lots of spice, but recommended reading order is below:

The Earl and the Vixen

The Rake and the Muse

The Marquess and the Earl

The Viscount and the Wallflower

The Duke and the Widow

Dearest Reader

Thank you for taking the time to read *The Viscount and the Wallflower*! I hope you enjoyed this spicy read from my Unlikely Betrothal series. I enjoyed bringing Alex and Lily's story to life on the page and can't wait to introduce you to the other couples at the Ockhams' house party!

I am so thankful for all my readers and would appreciate it if you would leave an honest review on sites like Amazon, Goodreads, BookBub, etc.! Also, I'd love to stay in touch, so please visit christinadianebooks.com to join my mailing list and receive a free copy of Only A Rake Will Do (the Ockhams are in that one, too!), and stay informed on upcoming releases, promotions, and current projects.

If you are interested in being on my permanent ARC team and/or Street Team, send me a message on one of my socials! I'd love to chat!

I hope all of you will follow me and get the latest happenings and info on releases from my historical romance friends on any of my socials:

- Website: christinadianebooks.com

- Substack: @christinadianeauthor

- The Desire Den Discord

- Instagram: @christinadianeauthor

- Facebook: christinadiane

- TikTok: @christinadianeauthor

- YouTube: @ChristinaDianeAuthor

- BlueSky: @christinadiane.bsky.social

- Twitter: @CDianeAuthor

- GoodReads: ChristinaDiane

- Follow Me on Amazon: Christina Diane

- Follow Me onBookBub: Christina Diane

- Join my Reader Group: <u>The Swoonworthy Scoundrels Society</u>

- Join my other Author Group: <u>Society of Smut & Scandal</u>

Hopefully I left you wanting more, so keep reading for a sneak peek at *The Duke and the Widow* from the Unlikely Betrothal series! I hope you are as excited as I am for James and Rosina! You can also go ahead and get your copy of *The Duke and the Widow* in paperback, ebook, and audio!

The Duke and the Widow

KENT, ENGLAND - JULY 1810

Rosina held her husband's hand, thinking back on the short, loving marriage they had shared thus far. It was unfathomable that illness could reduce such a strong, virile man to skin and bones. She would have given anything for some sort of miracle to bring him back to her. She pleaded to the skies every night for the last couple of months for some sign of improvement and any assistance from some other force that would make him well again.

"Do you remember our wedding breakfast?" His voice was frail compared to the confident baritone he had always possessed.

She rubbed her thumb over his hand. "Of course, my love. Some of my family is still quite scandalized, you know." She laughed, recalling the memory of the unexplainable grass stains on the back of her dress and the twigs in her hair. They had been so ready to consummate their marriage—not that it was the first time they had been intimate—that they thought they could slip to the gardens for a quick tryst and took a bit of a tumble.

He opened his eyes and looked at her. All the love he'd had for her on that day still shone there, and she fought not to let him see her cry. He needed to preserve his strength, so he might have a chance of overcoming whatever it was that ailed him. As foolish as she was to continue to hope. The doctors didn't know exactly what it was, but in the similar cases they had seen, the patients hadn't survived.

"I'm lucky to have been able to love you for the time we've had," he said.

They had been married for almost two years, but they had loved each other since their youth. Ryan, Marquess Preston, had been her older brother's best friend, and she'd followed them around everywhere. The boys were only a year older than her, and she made them let her go fishing and climb trees. She had always been a force to be reckoned with, and they didn't dare tell her no.

"I want us to go visit our spot in the woods at my father's estate," she said.

He coughed and smiled at her. The memory of the first time Ry had kissed her had always been one of their favorites. Rosina had been three-and-ten, while he was four-and-ten, and they were playing a game of hide-and-seek with her brother, even if admittedly they were a bit old to be doing so. They found a place in the woods where the trees formed an enclosure that they could just squeeze into. Pressed against each other, trying to quiet their ragged breathing from running through the woods, they stared into each other's eyes, and something happened. And she saw him differently than she had before. It appeared to have been the same for him because he leaned down and pressed a soft kiss against her lips. Her heart had belonged to him ever since.

"I was so nervous," he said. "I wasn't certain if you might slap me."

"When you are well, we shall go back there, and I will be the one to kiss you."

A frown formed on his handsome face. His features were gaunt, but she still saw the man she married.

"My Rose, you must accept what is happening. I will not survive this, and I must know that you are going to be all right when I am gone."

No longer able to control the tears, she allowed a few to escape down her cheeks. She used her free hand to brush back the sandy brown hair from his forehead. "We mustn't give up hope, Ry."

He patted the bed beside him, and she moved to settle in with him. He wrapped his once-muscular arm around her and she leaned against him. His body felt different, but he was still her Ry.

He married her before she even had a come out. His parents had been worried that a man of nine-and-ten needed to sow his wild oats, but he informed anyone who dared to question his love for her that his mind would never be changed. Ry convinced her father he was prepared to take up his responsibilities and provide for her. He forwent university and dove into learning about estate management at their country home, becoming every bit the marquess he was expected to be. He would be a duke one day, or he should be. Her heart splintered as she had never imagined that her beloved husband might pass before his father.

"You are going to have to go on without me soon enough, Rose," he said, pressing his sallow cheek to the top of her head.

They had been each other's first everything. Neither of them had even kissed another. Even when Ry was away at Eton, he remained true to her in every way. When she was six-and-ten, they began exploring each other's bodies. They had learnt everything about obtaining their pleasure together, with nary an inch that hadn't been touched, kissed, explored, or tasted time and time again. Their coupling had always been untamed and fiery, and then afterwards their embrace was tender and affectionate.

"I can't," she said, sobbing into his chest. "I can't lose you."

He rubbed her back, the same way he had for years, and she cried harder.

"You must, sweetheart. I want you to have a full life. You deserve love, laughter, and children. You are going to make the most amazing mother." His voice caught on the last word, and she hugged him tighter.

"I need you, Ry," she said, wiping her eyes and looking up at him.

He sighed. "I know, my love. If love were enough to heal me, I would live forever here with you, Rose."

He coughed again and laid his head back on the pillow, needing frequent naps the weaker he became. She lay with him in silence, willing the sickness to leave his body. Making every promise she could think of to whoever might hear her that she would give her very soul if it would allow Ry to grow old with her.

*****

Two months later

Rosina's brother, John, kept his arm around her shoulders as they watched the casket being lowered into the ground. Her family and Ry's had tried to talk her out of attending the funeral as women didn't do so. But she sobbed and went into such hysterics that they relented and allowed her to attend.

She had been with him almost every moment for the last couple of months, and she was beside the bed, holding his hand, when he took his last breath. She owed it to him to be there. But she wasn't certain how she would keep breathing once the dirt covered him and the only thing left of him was a headstone and the memories she carried of him in her shattered heart.

She moved as if she might step forward, and her brother tightened his hold on her shoulder. Part of her wanted to throw herself on the casket and go with him, but she knew it wasn't what he would have wanted. He wanted her to have a life and to go on without him, but she still couldn't fathom how she could be expected to do so.

After the funeral, they returned to the house she had shared with Ry. His brother, Rich, had become the marquess upon Ry's passing, but he was only eight-and-ten and intended to attend Cambridge before he took up his responsibilities.

As if she hadn't even been in the room, both families talked about her life and where she would live. They decided she could remain in the house as long as she wished since Rich wouldn't take up residence. She stared at the wall and did her best to ignore the conversation that only further solidified that nothing about her life would ever be the same again.

When the exhaustion of the day consumed her, she trudged upstairs and, out of habit, went straight to the bedchamber she had shared with Ry. They never spent a single night apart in their home, even the times when she slept in a chair by the bed. The sheets had been freshly changed and the bed turned down, but she couldn't bring herself to cross the threshold into the room.

She turned on her heel and went to the marchioness' chamber. Until then, it had only served as a dressing room and a place to keep her clothing. Rosina didn't bother to ring for her maid or to remove the black dress she wore. She kicked off her shoes and climbed into the bed, then hugged the pillow to her body.

Rosina wasn't sure how she was expected to go on in a world where Ry wasn't. She closed her eyes, longing for sleep, the only place where she might see him again.

Acknowledgments

There are so many incredible people—both new and longtime ride-or-dies—who have supported me on this wild writing journey. Authors, readers, friends, family, co-workers… you know who you are. I'd list every one of you if I had a few extra pages (and a really small font). Just know this: I adore you, and I'm endlessly grateful.

Steve: My husband, tech wizard, idea bouncer, chef, laundry hero, and all-around MVP. You believe in my big, bold dreams even when they sound like total chaos. Thank you for being my partner in every possible way. Love you, babe.

Dexter and Felix: My boys, my chaos gremlins, and the source of many laughs. You're excellent at distracting me mid-sentence, but you're also the inspiration behind some of the snarky sibling banter that sneaks into my books. One day you'll realize your mom writes smut... and I'll probably owe you both ice cream and therapy. Love you forever.

Rachel, Nina & Brittany: My mom, aunt, and sister—aka my built-in cheer squad. You've supported me through every high, low, and harebrained idea I've ever chased. You hold all my most embarrassing stories, so let's make sure you never talk to anyone without legal counsel present. I love you all dearly.

Erin: From the moment fate brought us together in the most unexpected way, we knew we were meant to be besties. Thank you for listening to every rant, dream, plot twist in life, and meltdown—and for always helping me find my way back to joy and clarity. You're pure magic.

Courtney: Fate handed me a twin flame in the author world. We literally finish each other's sentences (or just say the same thing) and have become legit besties. I can't wait for the day we meet in person. Thank you for our pretty much all day, every day chats, late-night idea storms, the pep talks, and all the chaos we've embraced together. We've got this, twinsie!

Morgan: The magic behind the scenes! You keep everything running, offer genius-level input, and somehow make it all feel easier and more fun. This book—and honestly, this business—wouldn't be the same without you. Thank you, thank you, thank you.

Bliss: Who knew a smutty follow train on Insta would bring me one of my dearest friendsies? Thank you for the endless texts, laughter, spicy scene brainstorming, feedback on my chaos, and all-around moral support. So lucky we found each other!

Rachel: You've read just about everything I've ever written, cheered me on, and gotten delightfully deep into this universe. Thank you for your thoughtful feedback and unwavering encouragement. So happy to have you on this journey.

To my **ARC and Street Team:** Your love, feedback, and support make my heart full. Thank you for shouting about these stories from the rooftops—you make this adventure feel like a party I never want to leave.

To **Dragonblade Publishing**: Thank you for believing in me and my words. I'm so excited to grow alongside such a passionate and supportive team, and be among your esteemed group of authors.

And to all the amazing **author friends** and **influencers** I've met through social media: You're one of the best, most unexpected blessings of this entire journey. Thank you for the inspiration, the laughs, the advice—and most of all, for welcoming me into this magical community.

About the Author

Christina Diane is an award-winning, bestselling author who loves to write super spicy, fast paced stories for the modern reader in the genres of historical romance and dark romance. Her historical romances are all set in the Regency era, with creative liberty taken within the historical setting to create a passionate, hot, intriguing story. Across all of her works, if you love combinations of high spice, witty banter, spirited heroines, forbidden romances, darker themes, and hot alpha men…then you are in for a treat! Because bad boys never go out of style!

She is a hybrid indie and traditionally published author with Dragonblade Publishing, Romance Cafe, and And You Press. She reads mostly spicy Regency romances and all shades of dark romances, as well as thrillers.

Christina lives in Northern Maine with her husband and two boys. Her family also includes their three French bulldogs who go everywhere with them, as well as two solid black cats. The entire family is always up for new adventures. When she is not writing or chasing after her family, she usually has a Kindle in her hand!

Her writing journey began at the age of nine when she created her own comic strip, Grizzly Grouch. In adulthood, she was a freelance writer for several years, mostly writing lifestyle pieces for blogs. She found that she couldn't stop thinking about stories and characters, so much that she had to get them on the page! Christina frequently has dreams of random character ARCs that go into a massive list of planned writings. She currently has more than ten series just waiting to be written!

Aside from her family, writing, and books, she loves Bridgerton, the Grinch, Jessica Rabbit, horror movies, Chucky dolls, cold brew, yoga, Hamilton, the color pink, and speaking in obscure quotes from movies and TV shows.

Christina loves chatting with her readers and talking about great reads, so please contact her on socials! She'd love to hear what you think about her books and what you'd love to see more of!